a Journey into Womanhood

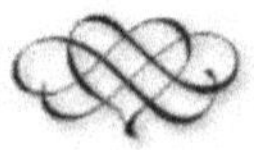

Coral S. Jocic

Proisle Publishing Service
1177 Avenue of the Americas, 5th Floor, New York, NY 10036, USA
info@proislepublishing.com

ISBN: 978-1-7362280-8-1 (sc)

Contents

I am a part of all that I have met;
Yet all experience is an arch where through
Gleams that untravelled world, whose margin fades
Forever and forever when I move.
How dull it is to pause, to make an end,
To rust unburnished, not to shine in use!
As though to breathe were life.

—Excerpt from Tennyson's 'Ulysses'

To my mother.

The greatest role model of all.

— C.S.J.

ACKNOWLEDGEMENTS

To my fellow writers,

Cheryl, Denise, Joy,

for their
encouragement, inspiration, and input
throughout the writing of this book.

Chapter 1

Joey sprang from her bed as the first streaks of colour flushed the eastern sky. She woke to the usual crowing of the cocks, and the familiar call of the laughing kookaburra, which the locals believed meant rain was on the way. Normally she would have rolled on her side, pulled the blankets over her head, and given way to sleep.

This morning, however, there was a restlessness inside her to be up and moving. She did not know why she felt this way or what urgency tugged at her so strongly. She heeded the instinct obediently. Somehow the day beckoned, holding a promise of excitement, surprise, adventure, or change. Joey went briskly to her desk, retrieved her much-loved diary and feverishly wrote down the words that now tumbled from her lips.

Spring 1950

'Morning Glory' Joy, happiness—
Morn tiptoed across my room, Blushing my cheeks
With the palest, pale rose hue, Awaking me
Tenderly, with dawn's first kiss.

J. McP.

Josephine McPhally, nicknamed Joey, was born in Cardellum, a small fishing and farming village that was down a dusty potholed road six miles in from the main highway. The inhabitants were few making their living from the land and the occasional fishing enthusiasts who came from the city sixty miles away. These visitors engaged the locals for deep-sea fishing excursions. The small town boasted one general store-cum-post-office, a rustic tin-roofed church in dire need of a miracle to make it presentable, a one-room schoolhouse, and the weather-worn houses of the residents. There was no electricity in the village as it would have cost too much for the villagers to bring the line in from the main road, so generators and kerosene lamps were used. Water too was a very precious commodity and rainwater collected in tanks was their sole source. But the people enjoyed their work, isolation, closeness to nature, and above all, the intimacy of village life.

Joey lived with her parents and two brothers in a timber-framed cottage near the azure blue sheltered bay where Cardellum had been founded. The residents were mainly descendants of early settlers from Ireland who came to this area with the promise of land, fishing, hard work, and ultimately, a brighter future than the city could offer these unskilled men. They were dedicated, determined people, and soon the land took shape under their care. Fresh fruits, vegetables, and a variety of fish appeared on their dinner tables and the people were proud. They did not grow rich as this was not the prime concern, but dug their roots into the earth and called this place home. They were not disappointed with their choice, for as the years passed, the children continued to nurture the soil. They married, gave birth, and died there. Many were related, but for all there was a sense of concern for each other, a need to help and be helped, to share the joys and sorrows of a close- knit group.

In this part of Australia, there was still plenty of wildlife in its natural habitat. Joey, with her brothers and friends, knew every creek, rabbit burrow, bird's nest, and of course, the best trees to climb. These were the favourites because the kids could hide in the leafy branches of these tall gums and be out of sight and reach. As evening closed in, they would glimpse koalas munching on the gum leaves and see the kangaroos out and about grazing in the paddocks. The kids knew many of them and would be able to get up close without alarm. In fact, the animals were quite bold and would approach the house for a tender shoot or succulent grass. What fun while it lasted! However, Ken, Joey's younger brother, would often blow their cover by running home to their mum crying.

'Mummy, it's not fair, the big kids won't let me hide up in the tree.' 'Which tree, darling?'

'The one in Mr McGinty's paddock.'

'They've been told before to keep off his property. Wait till your father hears about this!'

Of course their father did hear about it and they were duly punished.

'No pocket money for a month and extra chores on Saturdays,' Dad growled.

'Gee, Dad, come on,' the kids dolefully chorused.

'One more word from you and I'll double the punishment,' he replied sternly.

The kids shuffled off, giving young Ken looks that could kill as they hurried out. They knew better than to argue with their dad.

Joey made friends easily and had a genuine, if not naïve trust in humanity. She had rarely left her hometown except for an occasional visit to Melbourne to stay with relatives. These visits had not impressed her favourably as she missed her home and family too much to take a lot of interest in what the city might offer. She was a country girl. Often she would mount her horse in the evenings and take in the wonder of her surroundings. Riding bareback and with arms lovingly clasped around her pony's neck she would gallop with abandon across the paddocks, hair flying, cheeks rosy, and in perfect rhythm with her horse's strides. Occasionally Joey would yell at the top of her lungs, 'Whoopee! I'm freeeee, free as the breeze!' as she gathered more and more speed, until her horse, sweating and with nostrils flaring, began to slow down. Then together they cantered slowly home, weaving through the eucalypts in the gathering dusk, the Milky Way their canopy and guide. Joey would spend hours too with Ned, the oldest resident of Cardellum who lived in a storm-scarred shack. She was never tired of listening to his ever-fascinating tales of escapades when he was young. They were exotic and mysterious, filled with intrigue.

'You know, Joey, I almost got taken by a croc once,' Ned said one day. 'Good grief, Ned, how did that happen?'

'Well, you see I was up at the Top End makin' a livin' catchin' salties for their skins. Jolly good livin', I must say. Had good digs at a pub, the food was home-made, and I had plenty of 'baccy to roll me own. You know what I mean, don't you, love?'

'Sort of, but go on with the story.'

'Well, one night, me mates had spotlights on a prize catch. I was hangin' over the side of the boat ready for the kill when the bastard lashed his tail, throwin' me violently into the water. If it weren't for the others, I wouldn't be here to tell the tale.'

'What did they do?' cried Joey excitedly.

'They revved the engines, spun the boat around churning up the water, and frightened the croc off in the opposite direction.'

'And you, Ned, were you frightened out of your wits? Did you think you were going to die?'

'Yep to both questions, but me mates had other ideas. After chasing the critter away, they sped to me. By now I was swimmin' madly towards shore, but the croc wasn't put off and was hot on my tail again. Then, just as they were heavin' me aboard, I felt a tug on my right foot. Blimey, Joey, it was a near thing, and I even have damn big teeth marks in the heel of my boot to prove it!'

'Wow, Ned! Am I glad you're still here.'

'So am I, so... am... I,' came Ned's unhesitating reply. These stories captured and held Joey's interest for hours at a time. Then she felt once more transported back to reality and the security of all she had ever known or loved.

Joey was on holidays from school and was responsible for certain jobs around the house. This morning, she would surprise her mother by starting the fires in the old black kitchen range and set about preparing breakfast for the family. She loved the kitchen where the family gathered and where in the evenings they huddled around the radio and shared laughter and sometimes tears. Each family member had their own special chair at the big well-worn oak table, and protocol demanded you did not sit elsewhere. Dad, of course, sat at the head and Mum opposite in order to keep watchful eyes on their broods' table manners. Pussikins, their beloved Persian cat, could usually be found curled up on a rug by the wood stove purring happily away. Joey, like any teenager, loved to listen to the hit parade belting out the latest songs like *'Five Foot Two Eyes of Blue' or 'I'm Looking Over a Four-Leaf Clover'* until Dad could stand it no longer, shouting, 'Turn the blessed sound down before we all go deaf!'

'Oh, do I have to?' came Joey's pleading voice.

'Yes, you have to. Anyway, why does it have to be deafening?' ''Cause it sounds better.'

'Stuff and nonsense.'

'All right, Dad,' she muttered reluctantly but thought, when I'm older, I'll turn it up as loud as I want.'

While waiting for the stove to gather heat, she fed the chooks, calling to them as she got to the hen house. 'Time for brekkie.' At the sound of her voice, there was instant bedlam from within as each fowl half leapt, half flew from its perch, feathers flying accompanied by cackling and scraping. To add to this discord, the emerging hens at once vied for position in the pecking order. Then suddenly and without warning, the rooster approached! Strutting regally towards the squabbling females, his comb at full mast, chest puffed out with importance, and a spectacular display of black and burnt-orange feathers, there was no mistaking who was superior. The hens stepped aside, allowing the rooster to feed. Peace at last reigned in the farmyard.

This settled, Joey collected eggs and then went on to hand-milk one of the cows. She loved this warm full-cream milk that was now filling her pail, teasing both taste buds and nostrils, and she smacked her lips at the thought of the mouth-watering cocoa this fresh warm milk would make. Heading back to the house now with hands full, Joey was contented with what she had already achieved so early on this wonderful day.

When she entered the house, she could hear her mother moving the great iron kettles about and already the delicious smells of bacon and eggs filled the kitchen. She had not quite completed the task of preparing breakfast, but then she'd had good intentions, and after all, that's what really counted. With her basket of eggs and pail of delicious warm milk, she came into the kitchen.

'Good morning, Mum,' she said and gave her a loving hug and kiss. 'Hello, darling. What gets you up so bright and early this morning?'

'Oh, I don't know, I guess I just couldn't sleep anymore.' She did not want to reveal her inner thoughts or feelings to anyone now, not until they began to make sense.

'I bet you have a touch of spring fever, that's all.'

Was her mother right? Was this the answer to her feelings of elation and expectancy? True, she had been seeing a lot of Benny Bradford lately, in fact he was taking her to the dance at the church hall on Saturday night, but she had known him for as long as she could remember and could see no reason why this relationship should suddenly stir these feelings inside her. Then maybe the balminess of the spring air had played tricks on her emotions. Not to be deterred, however, from the feeling that something important was to happen that day, she began to set the table for breakfast as her father came in.

'Brekkie ready, Madge? I've gotta meet the fellas down at the pier in 'alf an hour.'

'It's ready, dear, but isn't Tommy going with you? Joey, go get that rascal out of bed and tell him that breakfast is getting cold. Remind him he's taking out a fishing party with his father in case he's forgotten!'

'I don't know', said Mr McPhally, 'what youngsters today are comin' to.

Why, when I was Tom's age...'

'Now, Jack, you know you're being too hard on the boy,' broke in Mrs McPhally.

Joey returned followed by Tom and her second brother Ken, and everyone settled at last to breakfast. Jack McPhally believed very strongly in silence at the table, especially from the children. This was a time for savouring the food before you and not an appropriate time for nattering. Besides all other logic failing, it was bad for the digestion!

Mr McPhally was a sturdily built man and craggy-faced due to years at sea fishing. He too had been born in Cardellum of Irish immigrant ancestors and had in his turn learned the pleasures and heartbreaks this kind of life had to offer. He knew no other trade and indeed had never considered another. He was aware of the many moods of the sea and had learned well how to cope with its sometimes-unpredictable spirit. His rough outward manner and strict behaviour with his children often disguised the true man beneath. He loved his family and wanted the best he could give to them.

Joey's mother, Madge, was strong-minded, determined, and a hardworking, devout churchgoer. She tried to raise her children to share her high moral standards and to live true to these convictions. She had little formal education herself and, like most women of her generation, had accepted the reality of a full-time career as housewife and mother. She had not resented, nor even disliked her role but carried within her breast the hope that Joey, her only daughter, might get a good education and ultimately a career before settling for marriage. Indeed, both parents shared these hopes and discussed them at length well after the children were in bed.

'You know that I want Joey to have a career?'

'Yes, Madge, and so do I.'

'You see, Jack, I think it would give her time to be independent, to get to know herself. I want her to have choices in life.'

'I want all our children to have the best education we can offer them so they can have career choices,' broke in Mr McPhally. 'Now, Madge, look at Tom. He's doing well at agricultural college. He's only 19 and has already shown a career choice and the independence to go away to college. The same you also wish for Joey, don't you agree?'

'Yes, I do, but surely you recognise that it's more difficult for a woman to achieve the same things. I was only talking to one of the parents at the school the other day who didn't tell her prospective employer that she had kids.'

'Why not, Madge?'

'For fear she would not get the job even though she was well qualified.'

'There has to be a better reason than that,' came Mr McPhally's quick response.

'No, just that mums are expected to stay home and look after sick kids, and that means lost work time. Naturally employers prefer to hire women without children.'

'Makes sense to me, but how does this affect Joey?'

'It doesn't at the moment, but I want her to choose any career path that she wants, which might be engineering or plumbing or...'

'Wait a minute', interrupted her husband, 'now you're really getting carried away. Those are men's jobs! For one, I wouldn't hire a woman, that's ridiculous! Anyway, I don't think we need worry about Joey choosing a man's job. I can't see that happening. She's not the type.'

'No, but just the same, I want Joey to know about all the possibilities, and I've discussed them with her. When the time comes, I believe she will make a wise decision.'

Joey had listened to her mother's words, taking them in with little thought in her early years, but gradually set her sights on a future that would be rewarding in the vocation she chose. Joey was now in her final year of high school, and so far, her decision on a fulfilling career was alluding her.

Like all parents, the McPhallys knew that if Joey chose to go to university, it would mean leaving home, at least, for a little while. Ken, the baby of the family, was still only 10, so for him at least Mrs McPhally need not yet worry. Secretly Joey's father believed she would eventually settle in her hometown and marry young Benny Bradford. Of his three children, Joey seemed to be the one to have her roots most firmly embedded in this soil. Indeed, Joey's future seemed predictable.

Wasn't she always the one to be homesick after a few days away with relatives?

Chapter 2

Later the same morning, after Tom and his father had left for their fishing trip, Mrs McPhally asked her daughter to pick up some supplies at the general store. Joey accepted enthusiastically.

This was the main hangout for the teenagers of the village, and they rarely missed an opportunity to meet. She rode her bike to the shop and of course ran into friends.

'Hello, Joey, are you going to the dance on Saturday night? I can't wait, Mum's making me this gorgeous taffeta dress with lots of tulle petticoats!' Mary breathlessly shrieked.

'I wouldn't miss it. I'm getting a new dress too.'

'Who's your date, Joey?' asked Tim. 'I wouldn't mind takin' you.'

'That's sweet of you, Timmy, but Benny's already asked me.'

'You know who I'm going with Joey?' chirped in Mary. 'The catch of Cardellum!'

'Oh, swoon, Pete O'Brien! Wow, all the girls'll be jealous of you. I bags a dance with him.'

'Don't know about that. We'll see. Got time for a malted milk and a Violet Crumble bar?'

'Always.'

Seated on the shop's front steps milkshakes in one hand and munching on the crumble bars, they greeted other friends who began arriving.

Soon the steps were lively with giggles and chatter from the teens.

'By the way, *The Heart-Throbs* are playing for the dance on Saturday,' commented one of the group.

'Oh really! The one with the gorgeous drummer? Hubba, hubba!' chorused the girls.

These encounters were usually innocent enough, and practically the only time these youngsters could meet socially without the eyes of their parents upon them. Even the many dances and socials that were held in the church hall were family affairs, with all family members attending regardless of age. If, of course, you could slip unnoticed out the back door long enough to steal a kiss, you considered your evening had been successful and satisfying.

For engaged couples, the standards were somewhat more relaxed and they would go to nearby towns to seek their entertainment. However, the respectable hour to return home was midnight. Any offenders to this unwritten law had better be ready with a plausible alibi, for on the following day, the whole village knew to the minute the time you arrived at your doorstep. The explanation was a simple one. Most of the residents owned some kind of car, whether it was a truck, an old bomb, or the latest model Ford, Morris Minor, Holden, or Hillman. Each one of these vehicles produced its own particular sound—*purr, hum, putt-putt,* or whatever—and as the returning lovers rumbled along on the potholed, corrugated roads, the stillness of the night was rudely assaulted, and even the heaviest sleepers woke. The owner was quickly identified by his car's own peculiar noise.

'Must be Charlie droppin' his girlfriend 'ome. No mistakin' his old bomb,' muttered a sleepy neighbour to his wife.

This was verified shortly after by the shutdown of the engine at the girl's house, and then start-up after a respectable pause. Quietness finally restored, the villagers were ready again for sleep, but not before they had satisfied their curiosity with a sly glance at the old bedside clock.

The young people accepted these norms of behaviour set by their elders in order to uphold dignity, honour, and respect in their community. Without these attributes, a family was shunned by its neighbours. Wild oats were most inevitably sown, but at a safe and remote location therefore, free from blame and scandal, or most certainly before their midnight curfew.

In spite of the illogical ring of these codes of behaviour, a standard had been set for the young and few digressed or strayed. They knew no other life and adhered to their parent's lifestyle. In their turn, they passed on these beliefs to their offspring.

So far then, the day had proceeded without any startling revelations or bizarre happenings, and Joey was beginning to feel her mother's light- hearted remark of 'spring fever' was probably a fair guess of her feelings of expectations. After all, nothing out of the ordinary had ever occurred in Cardellum, to her knowledge anyway. These thoughts went through her mind as she pedalled her bicycle homeward, passed old Ned's shack, waving to him as he suddenly appeared in the doorway, looking his full 95 years with the sunlight on his withered, parchment-like face. His hoarse, gravelly voice called after her:

'Come and see me again soon, I'm getting very lonely, and 'sides, I got a few more tales tucked up me sleeve that I'm dyin' to tell ya.'

Joey was practically out of range by this time, but waved one arm in the air to signify that she had heard and understood. She had every intention of paying old Ned a visit, as she was very fond of him.

She continued cycling, humming to herself as she wove her way along by the harbour wall, past the small wooden church with its cracking and peeling paint, and finally up to the schoolhouse, noticing as she did so the teacher's car parked in front. It was spring holidays and unusual to see anyone around, especially the teacher who usually took himself off to more exotic places. She pulled over to the side of the road to go in and say hello.

Although he had not been her teacher when she was in primary school, he taught her brother Ken and had been to her house for dinner, so she did not feel a complete stranger to him. He had arrived in Cardellum just a little over a year before, fresh from college, on his first teaching assignment, armed only with the optimism, idealism, and enthusiasm that is so openly displayed in those newly embarked upon their life's career. He was an affable young man, accepted readily by both the children he taught and the community as a whole. His sincerity and warmth of character, long hours of work at the schoolhouse, and participation in the affairs of the village earned him respect. It was no mean task to be the only teacher of children of all class levels. This needed a high degree of dedication.

It was the custom of small communities, such as Cardellum, that the teacher, if a bachelor, be taken in as a boarder by one of the families. He was a much-coveted prize, as the prestige of the family and its influence in communal decisions apparently became more consequential as a result. This was probably because the teacher was the best educated person among them and therefore duly respected. In time he would become their seer, counsellor, and most trusted confidante.

The ladies of the village, who had daughters of marriageable age, thought of him as the best 'catch' in town, or for that matter, for some miles around. They would go out of their way to invite him to dinner at every discreet opportunity, making sure that during the course of the evening, he would learn the many attractions and talents of the young ladies. He would catch onto their game quite soon after his arrival, but remain charming throughout the evening. If he felt, however, they were pressing their case too far, he would manage to slip quite casually into the conversation something to the effect that he hadn't had such a good dinner since he had spent an evening with his fiancée's parents. This usually would bring about an awkward silence for a short time, after which there would be some nervous clearing of throats. Then dutifully the head of the household would suggest a game of cards, or some such form of diversion; and once more the group was able to relax and enjoy themselves. The rest of the evening would pass without incident, ending on an amicable note.

It was not without reason then that Joey had paused outside the school before gathering enough confidence to enter. She peeked through the doorway to see the teacher, Paul Duke, a handsome young man, bent over his desk, seemingly too engrossed to hear her approach. A chalky smell drifted from the classroom, setting her nostrils a-twitch, followed by a huge *ACHOO*! Startled by this explosion, Mr Duke jumped up to see who his visitor might be and, then with recognition, broke into a friendly smile.

'Joey McPhally, come on in. What are you doing hiding behind the door like that? Is it because of your sneezy greeting?' He laughed.

'I was afraid I might be interrupting you and then of course I did.'

'Nonsense, I'm glad you dropped in to see me, I've been working on these lesson plans long enough, besides I was just getting ready to have a bite to eat. Care to share some sandwiches, I've plenty.'

'Oh thank you, I am a bit peckish. I was on my way home when I saw your car.'

Joey at once felt at ease with this friendly young man, who had made her feel so welcome. She couldn't understand why only a few moments before she had been shy about intruding. Now seated opposite each other at his desk, they munched on their sandwiches, chatting like old friends. As he talked, he leaned back in his chair, legs crossed in easy attitude. Joey liked the way his mouth curled at the corners as he spoke and his casual dress: shorts, thongs, and faded cotton short-sleeved shirt. Aha, he is human after all, she thought. His blue eyes looked straight at her as he chattered on, but she was more intent on observing Paul Duke than listening to his holiday travels.

'Joey, I've talked long enough. What about you at high school?' His unexpected words brought Joey to attention.

'Er, ah, I'm sorry, what did you say?'

'What have you been doing in high school? Which courses do you enjoy most, and any favourite teachers?'

'I love English, particularly writing essays and poetry, and my teacher is fabulous. In fact, I'd like to be a journalist and write for the Age newspaper.'

'That's a great ambition, Joey, but you do know that's a male-dominated field, don't you?'

'No, I didn't, but surely...'

'Please don't feel I'm deterring you, just making you aware.'

'Thanks, I will look into it. I also love biology and would enjoy working in a lab.'

'How about nursing? A lot of single girls your age go into that field.'

'I'd prefer to become a doctor. A paediatrician. But it's very expensive and would place a huge financial burden on my family.'

He listened attentively until Joey felt that he was like her 'father confessor' as she found herself telling him quite naturally and without hesitation of her hope to fulfil her mother's desire that she take up a worthwhile career. Also how she had not yet been able to make this important decision, and her worry over the short time left for her to make up her mind.

Paul Duke had remained silent throughout this, sensing an urgent need for Joey to express herself. Finally, thoughts spent, she looked at him with an apologetic air for having rambled so long. He reflected a moment, then said, 'Feel like stretching your legs, Joey? How about we walk around the playground and I'll tell you a few new ideas I have for the kids.'

'That would be great, love to,' came Joey's sincere reply.

They stepped outside to a flock of screeching black cockatoos overhead, an equally noisy group of kookaburras lined up along the school fence, and ominous black clouds were blowing in from the sea.

'There's a storm heading our way, Mr Duke.'

'We can sure do with some rain. God knows we need it, Joey.'

'Yes, Dad says we need the drought to break soon or the crops will be ruined.'

They were ambling their way across the school quadrangle towards a small tin shed when Mr Duke pointed to an area marked off for a new basketball court.

'How exciting for the kids. We always wanted one when I attended school here, and what's the tin shed for, Mr Duke?'

'Well, I thought it would be great as a potting shed.' 'A potting shed?'

'Come take a look.'

Once inside, Joey's senses were immediately aroused by the pungent aroma of oregano, parsley, sage, thyme, and marjoram that clung to every corner of it, beckoning her seductively to taste and touch. The varied leaf shapes with their differing hues of green cradled tiny drops of water, lending to them a freshness and wholesomeness.

'Oh, how lovely! You're growing herbs. Can I pinch a leaf of the parsley?'

'Go for it.' 'Wow, yummy!'

'We can grow them in here and then transplant in the empty paddock over there,' indicating it with his finger. 'Not only that, but we sell them too to raise money for things like basketball courts.'

'What a wonderful project for kids. I'd love to do that!'

'Do it yourself or inspire them?'

'Hmm, a bit of both I guess.'

They were walking back to the schoolhouse when Paul Duke stopped short in his tracks, forcing Joey to do likewise, then turned to face her.

'Ever thought of teaching as a career?'

'No, that is, not seriously,' she answered with surprise.

'You've mentioned your desire to perform a satisfying job, what could be better?'

'Well, firstly, I don't know whether I'd like being with children all the time. My young brother Kenny drives me clear up the wall some days, and then to think of maybe having to deal with thirty like him!'

Paul Duke smiled then said, 'Yes, but that's a very common feeling most girls of your age have towards their younger brothers. The relationship you establish with a class as their teacher is completely different.'

'Why do you find teaching such a rewarding job, surely it has plenty of frustrations?'

'Teaching children skills, guiding them to use their talents, encouraging when they are down, and helping them to formulate ideas and opinions all make me feel I'm doing an important job. A role that I thoroughly enjoy. It's often frustrating too, the feelings of helplessness and inadequacy when you fail to help a child overcome a problem, or when you can't understand why the maths lesson hasn't gone over as smoothly as you planned. You have disappointments in every job, but that's part of life.'

'You certainly make teaching sound appealing. I've never thought about it like that before. I suppose you get out of it, what you put in.'

'That's about right. Think it over, Joey, it could be a turning point in your life, and a decision you won't regret later. Also, as there's a teacher shortage, the government is willing to pay new teachers a wage while training, providing they sign a bond promising to teach for a minimum of two to three years.'

'My gosh! I will think about it, and thanks for listening to me.'

'No worries, it's been my pleasure.'

She took her leave of him, promising to drop by again, as soon as her mind was made up. While riding her bicycle home, she thought how strange life could be. Why, she had only stopped by the school to say a friendly hello, and here she was an hour later, her mind agog with new ideas.

Arriving home, Joey went to her room, where she could be alone and think about the discussion she had with Paul Duke. Teaching! This kind of work had never really appealed to her before, but probably because she was still a student herself and, like most kids, hardly wished to acknowledge that she might enjoy being part of a school establishment. Up until now, it had been fashionable for her, if not to dislike, at least to make a pretence at not liking, all those who represented power and authority.

Joey would like to help people, and what better way than teaching them something useful, firing their enthusiasm, and whetting their appetites for learning. What could be more satisfying? Joey knew, though, that in order to do this, she would have to be the exceptional teacher, her zeal never waning and her efforts tireless in order to keep those in her charge stimulated. These things she knew were absolutely necessary, not only because she had spoken with Paul Duke, but because of her own reactions and efforts towards her teachers. Some of them had been half-hearted in their approach with students, others vigorous and well prepared. In both instances, the children responded accordingly. Certainly there was no fooling the kids! They could soon detect the teachers who demanded nothing and, as a result, gave them little respect. Joey was wise enough to know that respect had to be earned, and that was the kind of teacher she wanted to be.

She lay on her bed, legs idly swinging over the edge as she pondered, if she could be the kind of teacher she so admired. After all, this type of job, unlike any other, was responsible for the shaping of minds and ideas in tomorrow's adults. A frightening thought to have so much power to wield over others; she would need to consider carefully before she gave opinions and set examples worth emulating, for small children would certainly copy her. If she could be all these things though, she would probably enjoy her work very much, even get to be downright enthusiastic as Paul Duke was.

The holidays too would be a plus, for these, she reasoned, could be spent at home if her job took her away. Joey knew also that her family would be pleased if she became a teacher. What more could a father and mother wish for? Their child employed in a steady job, safe from lay-offs, or economic disaster, an adequate pension, and even the training came with a wage. She knew that this would avoid any further financial burdens on her parents. Medicine, she would have loved but dismissed this as a financial impossibility, and journalism, if Paul Duke was right, was not yet open to women in general. In teaching, she could have security and stability, and a job that would always be in demand.

Excited by the decision she had come to, all alone, in fact, the first major one she had ever made, Joey jumped hurriedly from the bed in order to break the good news to her parents. The day had started with the promise of excitement, that something special would happen, and now the mystery was unfolded.

7 Sept 1950

Dear Diary,

Career choice made after discussions with my parents. Both were happy with the profession I had picked. Teaching it is!

J. McP.

Chapter 3

Joey was in her first year of teaching in a public school in Melbourne and she could not have been happier. The work proved to be just as challenging as Paul Duke had led her to believe some three years before.

Homesickness had been the biggest obstacle she'd had to overcome, but every holiday, Joey returned to Cardellum to spend her days with her family. Somehow these brief interludes helped her to cope with the separation from them and all that endeared her to her birthplace.

Until now, Joey had been staying with her relatives in Melbourne, but this was not really the complete independence she sought. She had been aided and protected by her loving aunt and uncle, and she truly appreciated all they'd done for her. They had eased her transition from rural to city life and helped to fill many voids. She had been introduced to a wider variety of people, taken to theatre and ballet, and travelled on trams complete with paper boys who jumped on and off the running boards shouting, 'Read all about it, read all about it,' while passengers fumbled feverishly in pockets and bags for coins to buy them before these boys fairly flung themselves off at the approaching stop.

The heartbeat of the city hummed at a faster pace, new faces everywhere, Greek and Italian foods to be had, and a never-ending variety of picture shows and news reels to pop into on the way home. The fashion boutiques along

Collins Street were a favourite haunt for Joey and her friend Amy as they window-shopped on Sundays, knowing full well that the price tags that accompanied the haute couture were well out of reach. However, slowly but surely, exposure to Melbourne was influencing Joey's palate, dress sense, and self-confidence.

For some months past, Joey and her best friend Amy Mantle, whom she had met in Teachers' College, had spent a great deal of their leisure hours walking along the piers of Port Phillip Bay admiring the great ocean-going liners. There seemed to be an aura of mystery surrounding them as they lay at anchor, brown water spilling from their sides. Their huge dark holds opened wide to a threatening sky as the immense cranes hovered overhead, emptying their contents unceasingly into the ship's bottomless pits below. It was interesting to speculate on where the precious cargo might be headed— China, Japan, Hong Kong, Tokyo, or Bangkok—or to what was in the packages and crates being loaded. The destinations held little reality for the two girls standing dwarfed in the shadows of these massive ships. They were no more than dots on a map representing another world.

Their attention was arrested one day as they took their customary stroll along the docks. There was an unusual flurry of activity among the dockworkers, and myriads of people pushing through the crowds to find porters, or dragging behind them oversized and most probably overstuffed suitcases.

'What do you reckon is going on, Amy?'

'Oh, of course! I read somewhere that today one of the P. & O. liners was sailing. I think it said the *Orcades*. Quick, Joey, let's go take a squiz and see if my hunch is right.'

This was a lucky break! Maybe they would get a chance to go on board, for Joey and Amy had never seen the interior of one of these 'giants of the sea'.

Amy's hunch was indeed right, for at Prince's wharf, the majestic *Orcades* lay at berth.

'Oh, Joey, I'd love to go on board, wouldn't you?'

'Would I ever, let's do it!'

'Quickly then let's get boarding passes.'

They obtained them, and being duly warned at the same time, they must disembark one hour before the ship's scheduled departure time, they scampered up the gangway. Here, they were met by one of the ship's crew, a gorgeous twenty-something male officer decked out in white uniform who dutifully took their passes and then asked, 'Which passengers will you be fare-welling on board?'

'Ah, which passengers? Oh, none,' came their stammered reply.

'Well, you know we generally only allow family and friends come on board?'

'No, we didn't. Oh please, we've never been on one before.'

'I'm sorry, but these rules only apply on the day of departure.'

'What if we promised to be very quiet and not get in anyone's way, would you then bend the rule? Would you?' entreated Amy, looking seductively at the young man.

Although taken aback by this approach, he appeared to melt and said in a lowered tone to Amy, 'Only if you give me your phone number for the next time I'm in port.'

'Oh, ah, of course.' And scribbling her number down on a scrap of paper retrieved from her handbag, she handed it to him. 'Thank you so much.'

'The pleasure's all mine,' he said with a wink.

'Oh, you bold girl,' whispered Joey.

'Well, it worked!'

Feet on deck, they were now in another world!

'Isn't this exciting, Amy? I'm dying to find the poop deck!'

'The poop deck! What's that?'

'Don't know, but I want to find out.'

'Oh, sir', called out Amy to a passing uniformed man, 'could you tell us how to get to the poop deck?'

'Certainly. Walk toward the bow, along port-side, climb the ladder, and you'll be there.'

'Thank you. Well, that seemed simple enough, didn't it, Joey?'

'You're really too much, Amy, asking all these questions. I wouldn't dare.'

'Only way to get answers. Say, Joey, do you know which way is the bow and which is port-side?'

'Yes, but not a clue from where we are.' 'That's helpful!'

'Well, I think it's that way,' Joey indicated with a nod of her head. 'Okay, Joey, you're the leader, carry on.'

They found themselves wandering along rabbit-like warrens below decks with cabins to left and right and with no idea in which direction they were facing. However, in their travels, they did encounter some interesting sideshows. On one occasion, they came across an open cabin door and peeked inside.

'Wow! This is like a luxury hotel suite. Let's take a closer look; nobody seems to be around. C'mon, Joey.'

'I don't think we should, someone might catch us.'

'Nonsense, let's go. Look, the cabin even has a window!' cried Amy as she went over to peer out.

At that moment, however, a cabin steward weighed down by luggage entered the suite.

'What are you doing in here?' Without waiting for a reply, he hustled the equally startled girls out into the hallway, just in time to see a fur-clad, diamond-encrusted blonde closely followed by a distinguished grey-haired man approaching. Joey and Amy stood staring as the two swept by and entered the cabin. Shortly after, the steward came out closing the door behind him and said to the girls, 'You're lucky I found you first. They are VIPs and you would have been in hot water if they found you in their suite. Anyway, what are you doing wandering around here?'

'We're looking for the poop deck and just saw the cabin open and went in to take a sticky beak. You see, we've never been on a big ship like this before and meant no harm, did we, Joey?'

'No, we didn't.'

'The poop deck! Well, it certainly isn't anywhere around here. Which way have you come from?'

'From that way,' Joey indicated, pointing behind her.

'Then you have to go back the same way,' he said crossly and sped away, leaving them with no further directions.

They continued on blindly until they came to a carpeted staircase leading to a deck above them from which they could hear lots of noisy chatter.

'Shall we investigate?' enquired our fearless leader of her friend.

'May as well, we're certainly not getting anywhere else very fast.'

On reaching the top, they discovered clusters of people, some with glasses raised, wishing a bon voyage, others locked in embrace, some laughing jovially while others wept. Amy and Joey wove their way through the throng, and as they did, snippets of conversation could be heard above the hubbub.

'Have a good time...'

'Don't forget to write...'

'I'll miss you terribly...'

'Harold, did you remember to pack enough socks?'

'Hurry back...'

'I can't believe you're all grown up and off to see the world.'

Amy and Joey took in this scene, and each wondered how they could ever part from loved ones as these passengers were now doing.

All too soon the loudspeaker system blared out its unwelcome message that the departure time was at hand and all visitors must disembark.

'Oh, Amy, I can't believe our time is up, and we haven't even found the poop deck.'

Laughing, Amy put her arm comfortingly around her friend and said, 'You'll get another chance to find it, don't worry.'

As soon as Joey reached home that evening, she wrote the following entry:

November 1953

Dear Diary,

I'm so excited after going on board the Orcades with Amy today. I can still sense the air of excitement, the promise of unexpected meetings and happenings once the steamer had escaped from the harbour, and was at home on the high seas. The mystery that surrounded the ship as she lay at berth invited me like a siren to step aboard and experience and share in her intrigue.

I'd love to make a trip, but then I wouldn't go alone. What if I was to get sick or lonely so far from home?

J. McP.

Chapter 4

Amy Mantle was a vivacious outgoing girl, who enjoyed most sports. She also had an adventurous spirit and had already made a number of daring expeditions into the Australian interior with friends, who shared her insatiable curiosity for the unknown. They had on many occasions tried to persuade Joey to accompany them, but she had declined, preferring to spend the holidays with her family.

Amy was used to leading an itinerant life. Her father was an engineer and he had been sent all over the country on different assignments. She had never really known the meaning of stability and a home. They had lived their lives like gypsies, moving every year or two, always renting flats or houses as they realized the futility of buying one of their own. For this reason, during her early life, Amy made few lasting friendships, and now as she grew older, she realized their value. When she decided to attend Teachers' College, she knew that this would mean the end of travelling with her family. Now at last she could begin to establish deeper relations with people and have a small flat that she could call home. She was determined to have what she had missed in her developing years. For three years now, she had been living in one place!

In many ways, Amy envied the closeness and warmth of family life Joey had experienced and the ease with which she could develop deep friendships. Somehow Amy felt she had been cheated of the most-prized possession of all—a lasting friend—and often as a small girl, she had wished so hard that she too might have a 'normal' home like all her schoolmates.

The pattern of life in her early years had left its deep-rooted effects upon her character, and although she strove to eradicate them and stabilize her life, she knew at times she was fighting against difficult odds. One does not follow a lifestyle over a long period of time to wake up one fine morning and be able to replace it with another.

Like Joey, she loved her work as a teacher, and this had helped to keep her feelings of restlessness at bay. Then, too, the trips she made during vacations had sufficiently quieted the gypsy to enable her to return to work with a greater inward calm.

The biggest problem for Amy at that time was how to handle the friends she had acquired in her adult life. She was both happy and afraid, for the moment she felt the relationship ripening, she began, against her will, to remain aloof from the intimacies their company offered. It seemed that instincts from within warned her against any emotional entanglements that must once more end in heartbreak and inevitable separation.

The exception in Amy's life was Joey. She was a stable person and a link to a childhood missed. Amy admired and trusted her implicitly and, strangely enough, did not recoil at the close bond that had developed between them. She could not explain this, but somehow felt that this friend would not abandon her.

Monday morning dawned clear and bright. The start of another week! At the morning tea break at Amy's school, the teachers not on duty were assembled in the staff room discussing the weekend's highlights with each other. Amy had been recounting to one of her colleagues, Helen Small, the movie she had seen with a boyfriend on Saturday night and then of her trip to the *wharves* with Joey on Sunday afternoon. With the mention of the word wharves, Helen interrupted Amy's dialogue, 'Speaking of wharves, Amy, you'll never guess what wonderful plans I have up my sleeve!'

'What are you talking about? For heaven's sake, tell me?' said Amy excitedly.

'I'm sailing for England on the *Strathaird*, January sixth, 1954. How's that?'

'My god, sounds unbelievable! Who are you going with, where will you stay, what will you do when you get there?'

Amy's questions now came fast and furious, giving Helen little chance to get a word in edgewise to answer them.

'I'm going alone, but that doesn't bother me too much as I do have relatives in England. I can visit them if the going gets too tough. One aunt in London has offered to let me stay with her, but I'd rather get a bedsitter on my own. As to work, I intend to teach just the same as I'm doing here. As a matter of fact, I sent my qualifications away to the London County Council for approval and have received a letter back confirming that they are all in order. After I arrive, I'll be assigned to a school. Now, would you like to look at a plan of the ship so I can show you where my cabin is?'

'Love to,' said Amy enthusiastically.

Helen took the brochure from her handbag, carefully unfolded it, and placed it on the table. Proudly she pointed out the cabin she would occupy, a four-berth one on G deck.

'Boy, Helen, you look as though you might be keeping the engines company, and no portholes. I bet it's as dark as the black hole of Calcutta way down there. Why did you select a cabin in the bowels of the ship?'

'Matter of money, my dear friend. The further down you go, the cheaper it is. I figured it was just a place to rest my weary bones at the end of a busy day. After all, I intend to spend all my time participating in the fun and games that supposedly take place on these "floating palaces", so why waste money on such mundane things as cabins.'

'Makes good sense, I guess. How long are you going for?'

'Oh, about a year. I think by that time I'll be glad to get back home.'

For the rest of the day, Amy couldn't forget the news of Helen's trip. Everything had sounded so exciting; she could feel that old restlessness stirring within again. Still clear in her mind too was Sunday's excursion over the liner. 'I want to make that trip just like Helen', Amy said to herself, 'although I've never travelled alone before, I'm confident I can. Of course it would be more fun to go with someone. Now who would go with me, I wonder?'

The natural one for Amy to ask to go with her would be Joey, but she knew what a task this would be to get her even to consider. This girl who preferred to spend her vacations at home and who was so happy and contented doing just what she was doing. However, she would be seeing her on Friday evening and could see no reason why she should not at least present the idea.

Joey arrived promptly at Amy's as expected. They were to spend a relaxed evening as they so often did eating a superb meal prepared by Amy, chatting together, and listening to the latest hits on vinyl. This, at any rate, was how Joey thought the evening would be spent as she reached the flat and pressed the doorbell.

'Coming,' called Amy from within as she headed for the front door and greeted her friend.

'Hello, Joey, come in. Oh, I love your skirt! How many petticoats are you wearing?'

'Three. I got them on sale at Myer's the other day.'

'C'mon now, let me see.'

'Okay, but let me get in first.' She then held up the edge of her skirt, showing each one.

'Wow, Joey! They're all beautiful stiffened tulle. I like the blue best. They certainly give your skirt the latest look.'

'I know, that's why I wear all three at once, but I take up a lot of room when I sit down.' Joey laughed. 'I put them on tonight just to make you jealous, Amy.'

'Hope you'll fit in my lounge chair, and yes, I am jealous,' she said with a twinkle in her eye.

'Dinner smells good, Amy, I'm starving.'

'I've got your favourite lamb cutlets sizzling away with mashed potatoes, peas, and carrots...'

'Oh yummy, I've got water in my mouth,' interrupted Joey.

'Let me finish, followed by rhubarb pie topped with cream, and of course, a bottle of red to wash it all down.'

Dinner finished at last, and both girls, feeling satisfied and slightly inebriated from too much wine, settled back in relaxed attitudes, listening to Johnny Ray crooning 'Cry'.

'Joey, I have something important to tell you and I want you to hear me out before you interrupt. Will you promise me that?'

Joey raised a quizzical eyebrow as she could not imagine what she was about to say.

Amy unfolded the idea to Joey detail by detail, from beginning to end, while Joey sat listening intently, absorbing it all. Her only evident movements were the changing facial expressions as the implication of Amy's words began to take on more meaning. Finally the tale ended.

'Well, what do you think? Isn't it the most outrageous, wonderful, crazy idea you ever heard?'

Joey paused momentarily before replying, 'Mmm, maybe you've got something.'

'Then you'll think about it?' cried Amy excitedly.

'Yeah, but that doesn't mean I'll accept. This isn't something I'd just run headlong into, but I promise I'll consider it and let you know.'

'Oh, Joey, I'm so happy.'

'Settled then', added Joey, 'when I've made up my mind, I won't waste a minute in letting you know, agreed?'

'Agreed.'

Fortunately for Amy, this proposal had come at a good time. Joey had a growing desire to really get out on her own and be wholly independent for a while. Of course, she had not in her wildest dreams thought of divorcing herself so completely from family and friends. Her idea had simply been to move into her own flat! However, Amy's idea had intrigued her, and this would, if anything, help her prove once and for all to herself that she was now a capable mature adult who could handle life in a responsible manner. Of course, she would not go if she met opposition from her family, but she doubted this would happen. They had always encouraged her to make her own decisions and would probably give her their blessing.

Living in another country, far away, and foreign, had never entered Joey's thoughts, as it had other friends of hers, but now that a realistic proposition had been made, she thought perhaps it would be fun and a great learning experience. What valuable first-hand knowledge a well-travelled teacher could bring to her students. For this reason alone, the trip would be justified.

The gains then, from such an experience, appeared to override any qualms she had about leaving her family behind, which were just childish and foolish sentiments. Joey decided she could find no real reasons for not going with Amy.

Their passage to England was booked on the *Himalaya* for departure, 7 January 1955, as they had honoured their two-year teaching bond in December 1954 and were now ready to take on the world!

Joey and Amy, surrounded by their families, were huddled together on the main deck of the *Himalaya*, saying their goodbyes as they had watched others doing a few months before.

'Darling, write often,' Joey's mother urged.

'I promise, Mum.'

'Take plenty of pictures,' put in her brother Kenny.

'With the new movie camera Mum and Dad just gave me, you can bet on it.'

'I'll miss you, sis.'

'Me too, Tom. Look after Mum and Dad till I return, promise.'

'I cross my heart.'

'Goodbye, Dad. Love you heaps.'

'You'll do us proud overseas, Joey, and bring home lots of interesting stories.'

'I hope to.'

The public address system told the visitors it was time to disembark. Joey and Amy now clung to their families as tears wet their cheeks and sniffles could be heard. Kisses lingered and arms remained close around each other. Although this was to be a temporary separation, for one and all at this moment, the feelings were of a deep sense of impending loss. As they began to move apart, their fingers still remained entwined in a final farewell touch, eyes searched their loved ones' faces to be stored in their memory till they were reunited. Then they were gone, down the gangplank, and onto the quayside. The families of

Joey and Amy stood forlornly on the dock, each holding one end of a paper streamer while they held on to the other.

Long after the gangways had been rolled away and the loudspeaker on the pier was relaying the familiar tune of 'Anchors Aweigh', and the steamer had left its moorings, both families still stood with the coloured ribbons in their hands. Not till these began to break one by one, and contact was finally broken, did they leave the quayside and begin to make their way homeward. Joey and Amy went to their cabin where Joey began to record *her feelings* in her diary.

7 January 1955

FARE THEE WELL

Ship's sirens heard,
The gangplank's up,
A puff of smoke,
A restless crowd
Upon the dock.

A wee soul stands
With tear-stained cheeks,
Sad and wretched.
Eyes meet afar
With her loved ones.

Coloured streamers
Clutched in her hand,
United still

By this final,
Tangible, bridge.

Ship's engines whirr, It sails anew,
The link is rent, A whiff of smoke,
Ship's gone from view.

J. McP.

Chapter 5

Their ship docked at Southampton, England, 8 February 1955, in the grip of a cold, icy winter. Dark clouds hung ominously overhead with the promise of more bad weather on the way. Not a very cheery welcome for the two girls, who only one month before had left a heat wave behind them in Melbourne. Their spirits, however, were far from dampened as they escaped from the customs shed to board the train, which would transport them on the final leg of their journey to London.

They had enjoyed their sea voyage on the whole, which pretty well matched their expectations. For the first few days at sea, they had found themselves pre-occupied with the tasks of learning to walk a straight line as the ocean heaved, pitching the ship about like a cork. In this early period of the trip, they discovered too who would make the best sailors. Joey failed this test miserably when the ship entered the turbulent waters of the Great Australian Bight, a well-known testing ground for the weak in stomach. She was not the only one whose weakness was made obvious by their failure to appear at the dining table.

Everyone too had their own theories of the best remedy for seasickness. Some insisted you should go on deck and watch the waves rising and falling. Others said this was bunkum, that, in fact, you should walk the decks, never stopping until you no longer felt nauseous; some, however, became sick to their stomachs at these very suggestions. Joey made straight for her bunk and stayed there until the seas lost their fury and were once more calm. She found this the best solution of all. Amy had no problem and did not miss one meal during the entire journey.

By the time the ship reached Fremantle, Western Australia, all had gained their sea legs, but to their horror, when stepping ashore, they discovered they were no longer landlubbers. Their legs were wobbly beneath them as they anticipated solid ground on which to plant their feet, long before it was actually there. Amused spectators watched their ungainly movements as they struggled to make headway. Oddly enough, most were glad to be back on board, where they were now able again to walk with ease!

The ports of call were probably the highlights of their trip, for it was here they felt their education had begun. When they disembarked at Colombo, Ceylon, Amy and Joey were appalled by the obvious poverty. Buildings were crumbling, and their doorways and alleyways housed the city's beggars, who were not only filthy and unkempt, but disfigured and mutilated by disease. Stumps of legs and arms remained, where disease had eaten the rest of their limbs away. The pathetic pleading in their faces brought genuine tears to Joey's eyes, and she spontaneously reached for some money in her wallet and put it into the lap of a deformed and wizened-up old woman. Next to gain their sudden attention was a malnourished, fragile, little girl who threw a frangipani at Amy, startling her as it brushed her cheek tenderly. Turning and looking down into the sad dark eyes of this beggar-child, she felt an overwhelming compassion for her plight, knowing too that the only thing she could give her at that moment was money. The child, now with outstretched hand, received the offering with a slight curl of her lips in gratitude and walked away. The girls knew though that this would help them little in light of their circumstances.

'How can people of better means hurry past these scenes of despair without so much as a second look, Joey? Could one eventually become so hardened and insensitive to the plight of others that you turn a blind eye?'

'Perhaps that's the answer, Amy. Let's hope that awareness of our fellow man will always be alive in us.'

Flies massed over the garbage-strewn streets and settled on the faces of the beggars who were too weak from hunger to even brush them away.

The Celanese, like other third-world peoples, stave off hunger pangs to a certain extent by gnawing on the red betel nut, which they eventually spit out, to stain the streets and pavements crimson like blood. Viewing such a scene nauseated Amy and Joey, especially because they were helpless to aid in any way.

They arrived in Aden at midnight, and to the complete surprise of the girls, the town was buzzing with commercial activity. Of course, the merchants would never close their shops no matter what the hour if a ship was due in port. Their livelihoods depended on the tourists. Open markets were set up everywhere, with the less-affluent pedlars carrying merchandise strapped to their bodies.

As soon as Joey and Amy set foot ashore, they were surrounded by these 'fortune hunters' of the night.

'Missees Simpson, Missees Simpson, lookie, lookie, bags, many bags, good price.'

'Why are they calling us Missees Simpson, Amy?'

'I guess it's because Edward VIII abdicated to marry her.'

'Oh, yes, and probably the only English name they know. Listen, they're calling all the lady passengers Missees Simpson. I bet the real one wouldn't be too thrilled.'

'Let's get shopping and have some fun, eh, Joey?'

'Remember, Amy, we have to learn the art of haggling over prices.'

Joey and Amy had been warned by a seasoned traveller on their ship never to accept the first price they were given. For in this part of the world, bartering was an accepted way of doing business, and no one but the foolish would contemplate doing it any other way. In the end, complete satisfaction was won by both, each believing he had received an equitable price.

They didn't wait long before they put their skills to the test as Amy showed interest in one of the bags and Joey tried on jewellery.

'How much for bag?'

'Oh, Missees Simpson, cheap, cheap, for you.'

'How much? How much?'

'Leetle, leetle,' holding up ten fingers, twice.

'Twenty! No, no, too much.'

'Good price, Missees Simpson, real leather.'

'I go look at other prices and come back if you are cheap.'

'You buy from me now, I give you good price, Missees Simpson,' this time holding up ten fingers only.

'I guess that's a deal,' she said as they smiled at each other.

Poverty also reared its ugly head in this seaport town. Some of the inhabitants were to be seen sleeping in the streets, on the ground, while luckier ones rested upon rusted, old iron bedsteads and springs, which had obviously been discarded by the rich. Twinkling lights from the mountainside pinpointed the cave homes of others who lived little better than wild animals.

Next, with eyes agog, both girls looked into a barber's shop in passing and were amazed to see patrons seated in battered old chairs having haircuts while others, for an even cheaper price, sat on the stone floor!

'Oh, Joey, can you imagine this in Melbourne?'

'Are you crazy, they wouldn't get a licence to operate.'

Men swathed in camel-hide goods and jabbering in broken English to the tourists was the way Port-Said greeted them. Once away from the quayside, however, the streets were deserted. They were silent, save for a couple of small food stores and bars, from which came the only human sounds. The remaining buildings were boarded and barricaded as if a typhoon were expected. Back at the ship, Joey learned there had been internal political trouble there when the British were no longer in control. Fighting with weapons between factions had become a definite threat to people and property. Some, therefore, secured their holdings and fled. In fact the Suez Canal was closed to all shipping in late 1956 and reopened in 1957.

The extreme narrowness of the Suez Canal surprised Joey, literally allowing only two ships to pass at a time!

Others waited in holding areas on either end of the canal, much like planes are kept waiting their turn when runways are all busy before taking off. Following along on both banks were sand dunes, broken here and there by clusters of palm trees, and a quiet, empty ribbon of a road. Not the most exciting scenery, but different, and for this reason, the girls were intrigued.

The Rock of Gibraltar looked down on them with stateliness as their liner weighed anchor in the bay. Once ashore, the two girls took a sightseeing tour and were amazed by the steepness and narrowness of the city's streets. These were eternally blanketed in shadow by rock and buildings flanking their sides. As the bus made its way, the driver, they noticed, constantly leaned on his horn. Everyone else did the same, in a show of frustrated effort to pass the numbers of lumbering ox-drawn carts, which blocked the constricted thoroughfares. Joey and Amy had not been accustomed to this kind of noisiness before and, in desperation, stuck their fingers in their ears.

On reaching the top of the Rock, they were immediately surrounded by well-fed, friendly apes, who appeared to be in better shape than many of the human inhabitants. The underlying reason for this was the superstition held by the British who believed if the monkeys were to perish, so would their empire! Reason enough for them to take good care of these animals.

The open markets, squalor, and the beggars seemed to have been landmarks of nearly every country they had visited. Joey was stunned by what she had seen and did not understand why or how such a climate of destitution and deprivation could be allowed to exist.

By mid-voyage, friendships and romances had been established, the passengers relaxed, and most appeared to be enjoying themselves. The days could be lazy spent in the sun, reading a book, or writing to loved ones left each day a little further behind. Some chose more active pastimes, participating in the many activities offered each day.

'Amy, feel like a game of deck tennis?'

'Sure, if you promise to swim with me this afternoon.'

'Only a short one, 'cause I want to work on my fancy dress costume. Don't forget we're going to the dance tonight.'

'You know, Joey, I'd love to try my hand at clay pigeon shooting too.'

'With shows, lectures, trivia, and exercises, I don't know how we'll fit them all in.'

Over this otherwise happy, carefree scene seemed to hang a veil of make- believe or fantasy. The atmosphere was conducive to romance and gaiety, blocking out the problems of the day-to-day world. All were aware that this unrealistic life would end as abruptly as it had begun when the ship docked at its final port. As the days dwindled away and Southampton crept closer, the frivolity lessened as each person prepared himself for the re-entry to reality.

The last evening on the ship found the passengers tending to their own last-minute needs. Addresses and telephone numbers had been exchanged, holding promises of future meetings. Lovers strolled the decks together for the last time, trying to recapture the nostalgia they had once felt. The bar- room regulars were swizzling down their final duty-free drinks, while others completed long-overdue correspondence or finished packing.

This superficial world was drawing to a close. The characters who had played their roles within it doubted that the brief friendships and romances they had enjoyed for this short interlude in their lives would be sustained or could flourish in the truth of reality. They surely must fade and vanish with the small world of ship-board life, as each parted the next day in pursuit of his own down-to-earth business.

Chapter 6

London! They had finally arrived and were now in a cab on their way to Earl's Court, a section of London, where, for reasons not clear, most Aussies gravitated sooner or later to form their own home away from home. Joey and Amy did not know this, for they had simply replied to an ad they had read in an English newspaper while still in Australia. The price had seemed right, and they were each to have their own bedsitter. Already they had observed many famous landmarks as they wove through the streets of the city, and it was difficult for either to contain the bursts of enthusiasm they felt. Everything looked exactly like pictures they had seen in the past —St Paul's, Houses of Parliament, Big Ben, Tower Bridge—and neither could actually believe they now were also a part of this scene, in the flesh, living it.

The girls were startled as the cabbie called out in broad cockney that they had arrived, so engrossed had they been in the sights around them.

The first disappointment came as they looked at 'their' house, and indeed the others surrounding it: row on row of unimaginative duplication. Each was of three stories with steps leading up to the front door, which opened directly onto the street. They mounted the old stone steps to see what unexpected 'delights' awaited them.

The girls were most pleasantly surprised to find their bedsitters, if not tastefully, at least comfortably and adequately furnished. Spotlessly clean with the smell of new paint still in the air and bowls of fresh flowers placed on their bedside tables in welcome. Each room was equipped with a two- burner stove, hand basin, and gas fire, besides the usual furniture items. Their rooms occupied the second floor with four other bedsitters, a bathroom, and telephone extension.

After showing the girls around, Mrs Reilly, the landlady, explained how to use the coin metres for both electricity and gas and unfolded the mysterious workings of the hot water boiler in the bathroom. She then invited them down to her living quarters, in the basement, for a spot of freshly brewed tea and a sandwich.

After such a warm reception from Mrs. Reilly, Joey and Amy felt at ease but a little guilty at their hasty judgements. If there was anything to be learned from this lesson, they must then keep an open mind and not compare everything to their own country.

Refreshed after their late afternoon tea with Mrs. Reilly, the girls set about the tasks of unpacking and making their respective rooms more liveable, adding here and there personal touches in the form of photographs from home, books, and souvenirs bought along the way. Their rooms soon began to take on character and cosiness, changing from austerity to warmth, places that would serve as a retreat at the end of a day's work.

Daylight was fading rapidly and the cold, damp air seemed to penetrate their bones. They dutifully put coins into the metres to give them both light and heat. Neither knew how long one coin would last, but they hoped long enough to see them through the evening. This might yet prove to be an expensive part of their budget.

Their chores completed, Amy joined Joey in her room to discuss whether to go out and eat, or bed down early, missing the meal altogether. They decided on the latter, feeling more tired than hungry. The next day would be a busy one, seeing about their teaching jobs, getting food, and finding their way about London.

Suddenly, there was a knock at the door. On opening it, Joey found four people, two men and two women of about their own age, standing there smiling. Before she had time to say anything, they chorused, 'Welcome to good old London.'

The accents were obviously those of fellow countrymen, and Joey was rather taken aback at this unusual reception.

'But how did you know we'd just arrived?' she stammered.

'If you'll let us in, we'll be glad to explain,' replied the taller of the two men.

'Oh, I'm so sorry', mumbled Joey, 'by all means, come in.' Amy had overheard everything and was sitting wide-eyed as the troupe entered. She couldn't believe they were to have company on their very first night in London.

'This is my friend, Amy Mantle, and I'm Joey McPhally.'

'Glad to meet you,' added Amy as her eyes met those of the taller man and lingered a moment before she lowered them in unexplained shyness.

'Meet some of the other occupants of the house,' put in the taller male, who seemed to be the spokesman. 'Mary

Miller, Joan Cantor, Jim Reeve, and last, but not least I hope, I'm Bob Grange.'

Introductions completed, they were invited to sit wherever they could find a place.

'I apologize for not being able to offer anything to eat or drink', said Joey, 'but we've not had time to get anything in yet. In fact we'd just decided to skip the meal altogether when you knocked.'

'That's already been taken care of,' said Joan. 'Mary and I've some baked beans on toast to offer, and the boys, some cheap plonk to help wash it down. Too cold for beer.'

'We're grateful,' said Amy, answering for both herself and Joey.

'Good, then we won't waste a minute getting it. By the way, do you mind if we eat here? My room's not large enough to swing a cat in.'

'Of course not,' replied Joey.

In a flash it seemed, all four had disappeared and returned with their arms laden.

Seated in a semi-circle around the gas fire to keep warm, plates balanced precariously on knees, the group talked, and munched on their food.

'How did you know we were here?' Joey teased, breaking the momentary lull in conversation.

'Mrs. Reilly's our oracle, bless her soul,' said Bob with affection.

'And there's not much goes on in this house we don't know about', joked Jim, 'in fact everybody's doings are an open book, so if you have any ideas of hanky-panky, you'd better think twice, 'cause it won't stay a secret long.' 'Don't let him scare you, girls', added Joan, 'although I must admit there's nothing private, living as we do on one another's doorsteps. However, nobody here's prudish, and practically anything goes.'

'But what are Mrs Reilly's views?' asked Joey.

'She's a broad-minded enough old girl to understand that single adults are going to have their friends visit in spite of what she thinks. So no points gained by trying to prevent the inevitable. So long as you pay the rent and don't kick up a storm or pull the place apart, she's okay,' said Bob.

'Everyone lives by their own morals, and that's the way it should be' said Mary, 'you're completely free to do as your own conscience dictates.'

'I'm just beginning to get a glimmer of how many different beliefs there must be,' Amy whispered to Joey.

'Me too, but how exciting,' came the hushed reply.

In the middle of this interesting conversation, the group was suddenly plunged into darkness, the only light now coming from the gas fire.

'Damn it', laughed Bob, 'the old metre's outta chips. Who's got some change?'

In the semi-darkness, everyone searched through pockets, but no suitable coins were found.

'I'll go see if Hardy's got any,' offered Jim.

'No, no', cried Joey, 'I'm responsible, I'll go. Where's his room?' 'First door at the bottom of the stairs,' answered Jim.

As Joey returned about five minutes later to her room, she was in a state of giggles. 'I've just seen one of the funniest sights, I swear.'

'What?' they queried.

'Well, after knocking and with a reply to enter, I saw this peculiar person sitting up in bed reading. He was wearing an old stocking cap, a scarf, and mittens. I've never seen anything quite so bizarre before, and it struck me as very funny.'

'Oh', said Bob, 'he's a Scotsman and as tight-fisted as they come. He reckons it's the best way to keep warm without spending a penny on the gas fire, says they're inefficient anyway. On this point, I must agree with him, you do toast on one side while gradually turning blue on the other. He's not a bad bloke though, except for his stinginess.'

'Anyway, did you get the coins?' asked Amy anxiously.

'Yeah', replied Joey, 'he seemed to have plenty and was most pleasant about parting with them as I promised to pay him back tomorrow.'

Light once more restored, the group resumed talking while sipping their drinks and enjoying each other's company. Joey and Amy listened with interest to the tales these newly found friends offered; after all, they were now 'seasoned' travellers, from whom things of great value could be learned about life in London!

Chapter 7

One week had now passed since the arrival of Joey and Amy in England, during which time there had been much to become accustomed to. The cold, dismal days of never-ending winter with hardly so much as a peek at the sun and smog blotting out the sky almost constantly. Snow had fallen too, and as neither girl had ever seen this white wonder before, they behaved like a pair of 10-year-olds with a new plaything! Out they went to Hyde Park and romped and frolicked in it, made snowmen, and threw snowballs—delightful stuff they thought, but changed their minds soon afterwards when they saw the beautiful white crystals muddied and turned to slush in the city streets. Snow then was for parks and other serene places, where it could stay in its virgin state enhancing the beauty of the landscape!

Both girls had wasted no time in making themselves known to the Education Department regarding their applications and were duly assigned to separate schools in London on the following Monday morning.

Catapulting down steep steps into the depths of the earth, Joey raced to catch her train. Once boarded, she wormed her way through closely-knit bodies to find an overhead strap on which to dangle her body during the jerky ride. At her destination, she was swept off her feet by the tide of her fellow passengers as they hustled through the door carrying her along with them till, finally, depositing her on the platform, they dispersed in a myriad of directions!

Today was Joey's first day at the London school to which she had been assigned, and naturally she wanted to make a good impression. Once she emerged from this subterranean station, Joey wrapped her coat around her body against the frigid air, took stock of her surroundings, retrieved a crumpled piece of paper from her pocket, and studied her handwritten directions to school. 'Simple enough,' she muttered to herself and, with confidence, noted the correct street name and headed forth with a jauntiness in her stride.

The school was located in one of the poorer East London suburbs. The small dilapidated homes sat one on top of the other row on row with no evidence of gardens or greenery as the houses edged the pavement with not a skerrick of room for such luxury. As it was winter, Joey noticed smoke coming from every chimney top and the thickening pall that filled the air. 'Where has the blue sky gone?' she wondered as she looked heavenward, almost falling into a chute, which conveyed coal to the basements of these houses. Curious, Joey peered down a dark hole, but quickly pulled away, spluttering and coughing from the dust. 'Phew! I need clean air,' she wheezed out loudly to no one in particular.

'You won't find it 'ere, luv,' came a reply from somewhere above. Joey swung around to see who belonged to the 'voice', but only the sound of a window shutting could be detected.

Glancing at her watch, Joey picked up speed as she did not want to be late on her very first day. Her high heels click-clacked as she traversed the cobblestoned street with difficulty, cursing all the while that sheer vanity had convinced her to wear them!

Tired-looking from grime-covered walls and age-weary, the school loomed as she turned the next corner. She stifled a cry of disappointment for this was not what she had expected. Soon though, as she got closer, shrieks of children's laughter, sounds of bouncing balls, and skipping-rope jingles could be heard from over the high brick walls surrounding the playground. Music to Joey's ears, which comforted her earlier feelings of regret. The kids had arrived at school, and with anticipation, she mounted the front steps and knocked on the headmaster's door.

'Come in,' came the friendly reply.

Joey paused to compose herself and with head held high entered.

The headmaster, Mr Pasley, stood up to greet her and, with a smile and firm handshake, welcomed her.

'Happy to meet you, Miss McPhally, Aussies have a great reputation for being very good teachers. We're fortunate to have you.'

Joey noticed how tall he was, the laughter lines around the eyes, and the kindliness that emanated from him. He's really quite fatherly.

'Miss Mcphally, are you all right?'

Joey snapped suddenly from her thoughts and stuttered, 'Oh, ah, ah, I didn't know that.'

'Will you take my word?'

'Yes, and I'll try to live up to it,' she replied smiling.

'Come now, I'll introduce you to the staff and then get Mary Banner to show you your classroom. You'll still have time for a cuppa before the bell rings if you'd like.'

'That would be lovely,' she said gratefully, as she had not eaten any breakfast that morning and thought with horror what would happen if her stomach started rumbling in class. 'The kids of course would love it,' she mused quietly to herself. 'I know I would have.'

Introductions were made over cups of tea, and Joey knew instantly this group of teachers would be great to work with. Already having warmly received her, they were encouraging in their efforts to make her feel at ease. Observing her youthfulness, easily the baby of the crowd, they also offered professional advice and support if she needed it.

Mary Banner, a plump mothering type who taught kindergarten, as well as other duties, approached Joey in the staff room.

'Well, luv, I think you'll fit in here. We believe in disciplining our students as I think you do in Australia too, so there's nothing new there. In your room, you'll find a good supply of old slippers in the cupboard.'

'What are they for?' Joey enquired innocently.

'What are they for, you say?' came her incredulous retort. 'Why, my dear girl, they're used for disciplining.'

'Oh!' said Joey, laughing. 'I've never heard of that. I think it's rather funny.'

'You do, do you? Well, you'll find they come in very handy when you have to deal with the likes of Johnny B. I can assure you. Come along with me now to your classroom.'

Walking briskly along behind Miss Banner, Joey took mental notes of where the gym-cum-dining-room and assembly hall were located as these would be used a lot.

'Here we are, this is your room. I'm just next door in case you need me.'

Joey noted that the classroom was set up for infants with straw mats on the floor, a Wendy House, varied hands-on equipment, scattered toys, large picture books, and colourful charts of all kinds.

'There must be some mistake,' Joey said disappointedly. 'I was not trained for this age group. How many students will I have?'

'About forty I should say.'

'Forty! Good grief, that's a huge group. I really don't know how I'll manage,' said Joey despondently.

'You'll do just fine, dearie. You are a supply teacher, so if you want to work, you take whatever's dished up.'

'Yes. I did know that, but...'

The school bell interrupted the conversation and she hurried along with the ever-attentive Mary Banner who was still clucking directions as they went on out to the playground where the students were lined up.

'This is your class,' she indicated to Joey. 'Put the ball down, Johnny B., and get into line at once. There, that's better', said Miss Banner in the same breath and, while pointing to Joey, continued, 'this is your new teacher, Miss McPhally.'

Joey looked along the line of children, and a wave of compassion for these little ones came over her. A poorer group she had not witnessed before with their patched and darned hand-me-downs, unkempt hair, runny noses, and little clothing to keep them really warm. She had heard of children being 'sewn' into their underwear for the winter and she could only think this meant they had only one set and washing them was problematic, for perhaps it would never dry in time to be used immediately again.

'Good morning, girls and boys,' Joey cheerfully announced.

'Good mornin', madam,' came the reply in unison, and Joey smiled at the unusual way in which they addressed her. Johnny B., who was shaping up to be one of those students teachers would gladly trade in, suddenly blurted out, 'You talk funny, madam!'

'So do you', came Joey's quick response, 'but we'll discuss why we think so at another time.'

Once in the classroom, the children settled into their seats. The school day had started in earnest. First off, Joey received a note written on toilet paper, which was thrust into her hand on her way into school that morning by an anxious parent. Later when the students were busily engaged, Joey had a chance to read the following: 'Please excuse my son from school t'day as he 'ad a fit of the back-door trots yesterd'y and I felt it betta to keep 'im 'ome.' Joey thought so too! How appropriate to write this on toilet paper. She covered her mouth with her hand and had a good giggle.

The next hiccough came when the students were asked to take bags of building blocks to the floor and then make shapes with them. Horror of horrors as forty bags were tipped upside down, simultaneously creating a minor earthquake. Even Miss Banner heard the noise and came hurtling through the door.

'Whatever happened?' she exploded.

'Oh, you heard it, did you?' said Joey with tongue in cheek.

'Heard it! I think the whole school shook.'

'It was nothing really. I just failed to tell the kids not to turn their bags upside down, that's all. So what you heard were forty bags being...'

She trailed off laughing at her own folly, with the children joining in the glee.

'I told you I'm not used to teaching this age group.'

Miss Banner smiled and gave her a wink as she exited, saying, 'You'll get it, you'll be all right, dearie.'

Recess came as a blessing and time to chat more with her colleagues. They were a diverse group of men and women with differing ethnic backgrounds. One little lady, for example, was Welsh and hard to understand, and a male teacher from Germany who spent his weekends wandering the country graveyards in search of opportunities to do brass rubbings. He offered to introduce Joey to this wondrous pastime, which she graciously declined, and of course now, there was Joey, an Aussie. So at this morning's tea time on her very first day, one of the Englishmen pronounced for all gathered to hear, 'Joey, I can hear that you come from Down Under and I can see by the shackle marks on your arms that you come from the colonies, but before long and with our coaching, you'll be able to immigrate back into Australia under the ten-pound deal. How does that sound?'

'Here, here, say all of us,' as the rest joined in.

'Very funny,' a red-faced Joey replied in good humour.

'Don't mind him, dearie, you'll get used to this lot, it's all just in fun,' reassured Mary Banner.

After the recess break, the children became engrossed in a painting lesson. The room was well equipped with a washbasin, most appropriate for this type of activity. However, twin boys in the class who looked like angels but weren't always insisted on doing everything together, including trips to the toilet. Joey didn't allow this, having enough wisdom to know what it could lead to. So she permitted only one at a time. Busy as she was with the rest of the class, more than five minutes had elapsed before she looked up to see both boys up to their elbows in soap suds. The soap overflowed the sink and slithered across the floor to the delight of others, who were in the throes of shedding shoes and socks. Losing her cool, Joey admonished the culprits by saying, 'What are you both doing? Look at the mess! You're all wet and so is the floor.'

'We're just washin' our hands, madam,' they said innocently and in unison. Joey exasperated, put out an SOS for someone to bring mop and bucket pronto! A lesson in counting was also noteworthy that day as the children chorused, 'For'y-one, for'y-two, for'y-three, for'y-four..."

Lunchtime rolled around not a minute too soon for Joey. She was not assigned to lunchtime duty, so she missed out on the free lunch the teachers received for doing this chore. The children were in single-file class lines, plates clutched in hands, and hunger on their minds, which could be seen by the expressions on their faces. For some, it would constitute the only meal for the day. They filed past tables holding large pots of hot food served cafeteria style. The food did not look appetising, consisting mainly of carbohydrates with little evidence of any meat. As each child passed through the line, sounds of sloppy food hitting plates was audible. Joey determined then that she would not touch it. However, the children ate with relish and went back for seconds.

Joey's first day ended uneventfully following a story and naptime for the kids. With the students now gone, Joey reflected on the happenings of the day. It had been an experience indeed. A learning time for her, but a rewarding one too, to work with these littlies who had endeared her from the moment she had set eyes on them. To top it all, she was in one of the more interesting capital cities of the world, London, what else could she wish for?

The weather was not the only challenge the girls had to face in their adaptation to London life. Heating and lighting of any kind was expensive, particularly as they were all controlled by timed, coin metres and then there was board and lodging at five guineas weekly.

'No more long, luxurious bubble baths for us, Joey.'

'Damn it, I do love soaking and watching my fingers and toes go all wrinkly.'

'Oh well, the end of an era not only for long baths, but also for going to bed in sexy nightdresses.'

'C'mon, Amy, let's not get too carried away.'

'I'm going to reach for a jumper instead of turning on the gas heater. The way Bob's friend the Scot rugged up in bed, so will I. It was definitely the cost that made him do it!'

'Amy, what if we have a fire and have to be rescued by gorgeous firemen and you're looking like the Scotsman?'

'It'll be my undoing, but I'm still going to do it 'cause I want to save my pennies.'

Quickly they both agreed they had to stay within their budgets of £469/14 per annum if they were to travel during school holidays.

They were indeed fortunate to be exempt from taxes for a two-year period due to the teacher shortage. However, if they overstayed their welcome, the taxman would come knocking to collect retroactively.

Caught up in the whirl of big city living, they felt an ever-quickening pace to their lives. This at first exhausted them, but gradually and unknowingly, they fell in with the surrounding tempo.

Both girls found many changes too at school. They agreed that the children were much more precocious in manner and speech than their Australian cousins, and although corporal punishment still existed, it was less evident here. The curriculum and class streamings, that is, where you group children according to ability, e.g., bright, average, and low, were completely new to them. They met these challenges, but not with enthusiasm. Both women believed mixed classes gave greater benefit to all. The Englishmen were something they hadn't bargained on. Wolves, the myths that they had heard concerning their reserved manners were soon dispelled after dating a few! This coolness then was apparently only on the surface, for once the barrier of the first date was behind them, they were as hot-blooded as hounds on the trail. Of course, not all Englishmen could be like this, but so far, these were the only experiences they had from which to draw conclusions.

'Amy, I don't know about you, but this complete freedom we have to do just as we please, when we please, and how we please is worrying. How about you?'

'Yeah, it's kept me awake sometimes at night thinking the same thing.'

'To be the sole judge of my actions is scary, Amy. So far our morals haven't been put to the test, have they? I honestly don't know if I can handle that yet.'

'Me neither. All I do know is this freedom is both welcome and frightening, and I hope that when I am put to the test, my beliefs will tell me what to do. I'm sure yours will too, Joey.'

The language in itself was no barrier, but the subtleties of British humour were beyond the comprehension of Joey and Amy. Spending some of their time at theatres, listening to radio, and watching television, the girls wondered why they could not laugh when everyone else did. After a time, they realized the punch lines they had been waiting for were not forthcoming, and therefore they began to listen a little more intently to discover the source for laughter. Eventually they found it, cleverly concealed in the text and, with this find, acquired an avid appreciation of English wit.

Every day was like the beginning of a new adventure to them as explanations of their new environment and fellow man began to take on more meaning. With each new experience and hurdle passed, they were able to dispel one more mystery, myth, or misunderstanding that had enveloped this city at the beginning. Little by little, they were fitting together the pieces of this complex jigsaw puzzle, with hope of finding the total picture and clearer understanding of London and its people.

On a chilly but clear windy day, the two girls set out early from their digs to explore the heart of London on foot. They twisted their way along narrow cobbled lane ways with surprises popping out at them like Jack-in- the-Boxes stopping them dead in their tracks!

'Oh, Amy, look!'

'What, what?'

'Do you know what this shop is that we're standing in front of?'

'Well, it's a beautiful old one, probably goes back to Dickens's time.'

'Look up at that creaking old sign, Amy.'

'Good heavens! Why, it's the Old Curiosity Shop. Quick, Joey, take my picture.'

'If you'll take mine too. I do love this cosmopolitan city filled with beautiful old buildings, cobblestone streets, and the traditions of yore that still persist. It's such living history. Vibrant—pulsating with life and ideas from every corner of the earth. You know I hated British history at school, but if I had come here then, I would have been more able to appreciate and understand its age. How about you, Amy?'

'Ditto, no history book can equal the experience.'

There were languages to be heard that the two girls had not known existed.

'Gee, Joey, we both learned French and German in school, but all the dialects spoken by just the Indian population in London is mind-boggling, never mind all the other nationalities.'

'I know. I remember as a kid if I heard an American accent on the street, I was spellbound. After all, that was heard only at the pictures.'

'Yeah, but we do have Italians and they are introducing us to a different culture and foods as do the Greeks, but most of us don't eat out much. At home we just mainly eat meat and three veggies for dinner.'

At the flea markets, with old and new goods brushing sides, Joey and Amy jostled shoulder to shoulder with the crowds. Among them were the Pearly Kings and Queens, so named for their pearl-button bedecked costumes. All were headed for the bargain tables.

'Amy, I've just found the most gorgeous necklace, silver filigree set with amethysts.'

'Bet it's not as gorgeous as my pearl-drop earrings,' she teased, screwing them on deftly.

London was museums, art galleries, theatres, and cinemas to fit every pocket, age, and taste. This surely must be the hub of the world. Where else could one find so much variety and in so little time try to satisfy the urge to see it all—not to be cheated of the next surprise waiting round the corner?

Of course the task was an impossible one, but their leisure times were crammed just the same in order to take advantage of every opportunity that presented itself for further exploration. They had rented a car during Easter holidays and travelled north to Scotland, marvelling at its many castles and black-faced sheep—with tails. A sight not seen back home. Then across to Ireland by ferry where Amy asked directions of a local and his reply: 'Now you see that road, don't take it, and you see that one, don't take it either, take the other one.'

Next they headed back through Wales with its unpronounceable names to London.

They didn't absorb much on these trips, for they were too hurried, but were happy they had been able to at least glimpse them and bring back some impressions, hopefully lasting ones.

Chapter 8

Joey had little time during these first few months in England to give much thought to home, least of all feel any pangs of homesickness. In fact she was proud of the way she was conducting her life and keeping her emotions under control. True waves of nostalgia passed over her each time she received a letter from Australia, giving news of friends and relatives. However, these proved to be momentary, as she did not panic nor desire to be on the next ship heading home. Life here was proving to be the greatest lesson she had so far been exposed to, and to throw this up now, for the sake of sentimental whims, would have been foolish to say the least. This was a once-in-a-lifetime opportunity and she was determined to see the year through.

Amy had been dating Bob Grange almost from their first meeting, the two having been instantly attracted to each other. The romance had blossomed and shown promise of a bright future. However, Amy became moody as she felt the relationship taking on new dimensions. She knew they were falling in love, and her instinct was to retreat before the situation got out of hand. Desperately she searched her heart and soul for a solution.

Bob could not understand why Amy was behaving as she did. They had got along so well together and enjoyed each other's company to the point of being almost inseparable. Then, for no reason clear to Bob, Amy had turned a cold shoulder.

He was a sincere man and had treated Amy from the first with respect. No demands had been made of her to make love, for he realized she was a virgin. He did not want to be the one to take advantage of her innocence and later be responsible for her feelings of guilt.

Serious about his intentions towards her and sure of his love, he had intended to ask Amy to marry him. He had a good job with a large engineering company; indeed it was due to them that he was now in England. The Australian branch had sent him to London to get some on-the-spot training with the head firm, assuring Bob of a good promotion on his return to Melbourne in December. With this in mind, he had felt in a position to contemplate marriage. Now he was having second thoughts! He had believed she loved him too, but her actions of late gave him feelings to the contrary.

He had pleaded and begged Amy to tell him what was wrong, but she had shrugged him off by saying it was something over which she had no control. This was no answer, and he was more perplexed than ever. Could this be the girl he thought he knew and loved so well?

Turning at last to the only person who might be able to throw some light on the mystery, he knocked on Joey's door. From within came the cheery answer, 'Come in.'

'Hello, Joey, hope I'm not disturbing you?'

'No, I'm just reading the paper. Here, make yourself comfortable. Hey, why so glum-looking, nothing serious I hope?'

'As a matter of fact, I'm not feeling exactly on top of the world.' 'Out with it. What can I do to help?'

'Well, it's about Amy.'

'I might have guessed,' quipped Joey amiably. 'She's not been looking too happy herself lately. You two had a fight or something?'

'No, and that's the most puzzling thing of all. If we had, I wouldn't be here to ask your help, everything would be clear.'

'Whatever are you talking about, Bob?'

'Amy's been avoiding me lately, and as I can see no reason for such behaviour, I thought you could tell me something I don't know. Can you cast any light on what might be wrong?'

'Haven't you asked Amy herself for a reason?'

'Of course, but with no satisfactory reply. She just mumbled something about having no control over her actions. Maybe you can explain what she meant by that.'

'Oh, I get it', sighed Joey, 'that same problem.'

'Tell me for Pete's sake, if there's a problem, I want to do my best to help.'

'Okay, I'll tell you about it, as well as I can.'

Joey related to Bob the childhood grief Amy had suffered in not being able to sustain lasting friendships due to her nomadic life. The indelible pain she had felt when each budding friendship was cut before maturity. How she had learned to prevent herself from facing further agony by avoiding close relationships altogether and finally running from the problems, using travel as her scapegoat, and an excuse for not having the thing she so desperately wanted, but felt inept to handle.

'My god', breathed Bob, 'I had no idea that Amy was going through so much. She's afraid I'll ditch her, and she's trying to protect herself the only way she knows how. Gee, you've certainly helped me understand her attitude better, Joey. All I want to do is show her that not all friendships have to end.'

'It'll take some patience and understanding, Bob.'

'She wasn't afraid of getting close to you, Joey, how do you explain that?'

'I don't know, but I'll bet once she's made to feel secure, you'll have no more problems.'

'Thanks, Joey. I feel better, it's not as bad as I'd imagined. I'm off to see her now, and this time I won't go till she tells all. That seems the only way to help her.'

Bob left and Joey heard his footsteps in the hallway heading in the direction of Amy's room. With the love he had for her, Joey knew Amy's running days were almost over. Her door was open, so Bob went in without bothering to knock.

'How's my best girl?' he asked, taking Amy by surprise.

'Oh you nitwit, Bob, you scared the life out of me,' she admonished him. 'Come over here, darling, sit on my knee', he said playfully, 'then I want to know why you've been purposely avoiding me, hmm.'

'Avoiding you, nonsense! I've been busy, that's all,' she replied, not budging from her chair.

Seeing she would not come to him, Bob slid onto another seat facing her. 'Too busy! For about twenty-four hours of every day, for about the last two weeks. Come on, Amy, don't play games. I know you better than that. It's this thing that you have no control over, right?'

'You've been talking with Joey, I'll bet. Why I'll...'

'Yes, as a matter of fact, but don't blame her. I went for some answers that you wouldn't give.'

'Well, I hope you're satisfied?'

'No, as a matter of fact, I'm not! Can we please stop all this pretending, Amy? This time I won't leave till we've had this out, and then if you still don't want to see me, I won't bother you again. Is that fair?'

'I suppose so', she said unconvincingly, 'but wouldn't it be easier if you just went away now and forgot that we ever met?'

'I guess so, but that wouldn't solve anything, and besides I love you, silly, and that's the real reason for being here.'

'That's just the problem, Bob, I can't handle our love, and I'm frightened.'

'But, Amy, there's nothing to be afraid of.'

'That's easy for you to say, you haven't been hurt like I have.'

'Probably true, but that's no reason to chicken out. God only knows, Amy, life is full of hurts, but we can't escape forever from ourselves. You'll just have to gamble on the outcome.'

'But, Bob, I don't want to let myself love you too much, because I'd die inside if you went away. Don't you understand I can't let that happen—I won't have that happen?'

'Why, Amy, do you assume all the time that it won't last?'

'It never has before, so why should it now?' she said angrily.

'That was because you were constantly moving around, no fault of yours.

Now you're in charge of your life, so why are you persecuting yourself?'

'What do you mean by that?'

'Well then, what was the real motive for this trip? To see the world, or escape from your self-imposed problem?'

'If I'm honest, I'd have to say escape, but that doesn't mean I regret coming,' she hurriedly added.

'No, no, of course not, but it was the stimulus. So why not settle down at last?'

'Settle down?' she said, puzzled.

'What I'm trying to say, Amy, is, will you marry me?'

'Marry you! I didn't expect this. Are you serious, Bob?'

'Of course I am. Been contemplating it for a while as a matter of fact. So you see, darling, I had no intention of leaving you.'

'Give me some time to think it over.'

'I'd like your answer now, Amy.'

'I can't, Bob, not now, I'm not sure.'

'When then?' Bob asked impatiently.

'As soon as I return from summer holidays, I promise.'

Chapter 9

It was six on a warm evening in summer as Joey and Amy disembarked from their channel steamer at Ostend. The beginning of their five-week summer vacation and they were to spend it hitch-hiking through Europe! Their friends in London had warned them of the risks involved in such an escapade, but they ignored them. The one concession they did make, however, was the promise to hitch rides with only one person, for safeties' sake. Bob had shown particular concern, but Amy pledged they would take no undue risks and would write regularly to keep him posted of their welfare.

Here they were then, each equipped with only a small duffel bag slung over a shoulder and maps in hand. They had decided to travel with as few items as possible to make their trek less burdensome, for they didn't know how far they must walk before some kind-hearted soul would pick them up. They hoped to reach Brussels the same evening and take advantage of a good night's sleep at the youth hostel there. They'd found these places inexpensive and clean on their trips through the British Isles and now intended to make use of them again in Europe.

Standing now at the kerbside, and feeling somewhat foolish and embarrassed about their proposed actions, they presented a picture of helplessness to the casual eye, neither girl wanting to be the one to perform the audacious act first. They had already allowed several cars to slip by them, as they timidly clung to the grassy edges of the road.

This would never do, they decided, if they wanted to reach to their destination that evening!

They agreed to take turns in thumbing a ride. After flipping a coin to determine who would go first, Joey stepped closer to the roadway to take up her post. She had lost the toss! Raising her thumb in a most unprofessional manner, to the accompaniment of giggles from Amy, she posed in readiness for her first target. She did not have to wait long, for this was a busy highway. She could already see the approaching car housed one person only and began wiggling her thumb wildly, lest it should not been seen. The car passed, but as it did so, a screech of brakes could be heard, and it rolled to a standstill several yards away. Overjoyed by their instant success, the girls swept up their duffel bags, which only a few moments before they had placed at the side of the road in anticipation of maybe a long wait and raced towards the waiting car.

Since the license plates were French, the girls decided it would be appropriate to address the driver in this tongue, that is, the little they knew of it.

'Parlez-vous Francais?' asked Joey.

'Mais oui,' came the reply.

'Allez-vous donc a Bruxelles?' queried Amy.

'Certainement,' he answered.

It was not until they were halfway to Brussels that Joey and Amy discovered their chauffeur spoke English. In the excitement, they had failed to ask this obvious question, and the trouble they had to keep the conversation alive in French, only God and themselves would ever know. Finally, they were set down at the door of the youth hostel. They thanked the kind man profusely and were lucky enough to find a room despite the lateness of the hour.

The dormitory was musty-smelling and consisted of about twenty double- decker berths, all of which appeared to be occupied. Most of the women had already retired for the night, and heavy breathing and the occasional snore were the only sounds to penetrate the stillness. Quickly and quietly, so as not to disturb those already sleeping, Joey and Amy prepared for bed.

Joey was abruptly shaken from her sleep the next morning by convulsive movements of her bunk. She sat bolt upright, not remembering at first where she was, to be greeted by two stockinged feet dangling from the upper berth in readiness for a plunge to the floor. The bunk swayed violently as the upper occupant at last swung herself loose, and the floorboards resounded as she finally made contact.

Joey glanced at her watch in disbelief as she saw the time standing at 5:00 a.m. Early starts were commonplace among hitch-hikers, but this was ridiculous! She groaned, rolled on her side, and prepared to fall asleep again, when the echo of heavy army boots assaulted her ears. Peeking from under one sleepy eyelid to see the culprit of this newest crime, she saw 'her', an ungainly, heavy-set young woman with dishevelled blond hair bent almost double beneath the largest knapsack imaginable. Dressed in faded old jeans, army jacket, and hobnailed boots, this girl seemed bent on conquering all of Europe on foot! By now everyone had been awakened by this fracas and seemed resigned to the fact that more sleep was now an impossibility.

One by one they left the cosiness of their beds and set about the tasks of readying themselves for the hard day ahead. Some hoped to be covering long distances, while others like Joey and Amy would have a more relaxed day of sightseeing, returning again to spend one more night in this hostel. They were of all nationalities, from all walks of life speaking a variety of languages, yet they shared a spirit of adventure, to see Europe, if not the most luxurious way, the fun way!

So far their journey had progressed smoothly, the two finding little difficulty in getting lifts along the route, as they adhered to the main highways, where traffic was in constant flow. They had travelled through Belgium and were impressed by the cleanliness and orderliness of its streets, the quaintness of thatched-roofed cottages on the outskirts of the towns, and the business-like manner in which the locals went about their day-to-day work.

'I've always loved the wonderful straw-roofed houses, just like Anne Hathaway's place. Remember, Joey, the goat we saw on the roof of a thatched barn in England?'

'Yeah, that was not a scene you'd ever see at home, but in perfect harmony here.'

Luxembourg was a fairyland with castles to match its make-believe mood. Here the two spent the night in the grandeur of a turret room. Indeed, this time the youth hostel had extended its welcome to the bedraggled by offering them a superb chateau, complete with moat and drawbridge!

This place reminds me of the castles you see in fairy tales and I actually feel like a princess waiting to be carried off by my charming prince.'

'Well, hold the fantasy, Cinderella, 'cause I don't think it'll last much past midnight,' chuckled Amy.

It was not until our travellers reached Switzerland that they began to know what high mountains were really like. In Australia, Mt. Kosciusko, the tallest mountain, at some seven thousand feet, would have appeared no more than a mere foothill among these giants. Amy and Joey craned their necks to see the elevated peaks, but were foiled in their efforts as these were wrapped in eddying mists. The girls marvelled at the secrets these venerable, masked summits must surely conceal!

From the grandeur that loomed above them, there came in sharp contrast the peacefulness within the valleys and lakes at their feet. Jingling bells echoed through the tranquil glens. The Aussies at first listened to these peals. They had never heard such sounds before, for back home the animals certainly wouldn't wear chimes. Why then the need for them here? Their driver of the moment explained, 'How else could you find them up there among those crags?'

The Swiss towns were quaint, decked out with profusely blooming plants embedded in cheerily painted window boxes, which adorned every building, no matter how humble. The cafes and public houses were impeccably clean, from their white-starched tablecloths to their uniformed waitresses. The pathways were even scrubbed sterile as hospital wards! Nowhere did the girls see any litter at all. How different from practically every other place they had visited. Yet somehow they missed that little grubbiness that gives a feeling of vibrancy and life. The total austerity made them uncomfortable. They got the feeling they should only look, but not touch, lest they sully this unreal environment.

Italy—Venice with its reeking canals, and the once-beautiful art galleries, cathedrals, the Doge's palace, and Bridge of Sighs, which adorned their sides—now replaced by cracking walls, peeling paint and lopsidedness, showing the eventual surrender of an era passed to the hands of decay. Intrigue, however, still lingered in her alleyways and thoroughfares where lovers met at dusk and clandestine deals were made, gaiety in her squares and night spots, love in her gondolas, and tranquillity within her many churches. Joey and Amy abhorred the stench, which invaded every part of the city, but stayed and endured it. They had found her charms too many to ignore and had gone in pursuit of them.

Their final night in Venice was in the company of two charming Italians: for Joey and Amy had found these men charming indeed! Hair slicked back with shiny oil, swarthy skinned, and suited up in white pants, jacket, and shoes, complemented by pale blue shirts, they looked irresistible and more than ready for a night of amore. Showered with attention, the girls were wined and dined to excess and made to feel feminine, desirable, bella, and sensuous. Now the stage was set for the final seduction. Using flamboyant gestures and the local dialect, the Romeos went into action. Nonplussed, the girls looked at each other and giggled.

'Non comprendo,' Amy said, still giggling.

Pointing to his heart, Gino, who fancied Amy, said quickly, 'Amori, questa sera, Lido, si?'

Knowing full well the gist of Gino's words, Amy decided to have some fun.

'Non comprendo, ripeta, adagio per favore.'

Gino repeated his question, this time joined by Franco, who had the hots for Joey.

'Bella, bella Lido dolce, gondola,' indicating the direction of the Lido, which was just outside the port of Venice.

A still giggling Joey asked, 'what do you think, Amy, the night is still young?'

'Well, if nothing else, it will be an adventure, something we'll probably tell our grandkids about one day.'

Their light-headedness prevented the ring of any warning bell! Once on the strand, the two young men decided the time had come for pairing off. Even through their fuzziness, the girls now became alarmed and objected strongly. Not to be deterred however from their evening's plan, the men drew them closer in passionate embrace.

A fight ensued with Joey and Amy using all their female strength and guile to keep the men at arm's length. Freed from their clutches at last, they sped off in the direction of the ferry, pursued by less enthusiastic and somewhat crestfallen lovers.

On reaching the quayside, they were dismayed to learn that the last ferry of the evening had departed, the next scheduled for six in the morning! This was a predicament they had not counted on, and it meant they must spend the rest of the night warding off the amorous advances of their two escorts.

They were mistaken, however, for the Italians had never been rebuffed in this way before. Their pride was sorely hurt, and their manliness put in jeopardy, for they fancied themselves as seducers, not rapists, and no longer desired such unwilling partners.

Joey and Amy left Venice and the two young men, a little wiser they hoped, and better prepared for any future entanglements of this nature.

Stuck one day on a small country road on their way to Pisa, the two suddenly found themselves the centre of curiosity and attention by the local villagers as it was not every day that young women were seen hitch-hiking on this stretch of road. One moment they were alone, the next surrounded by a friendly, staring crowd.

The local police even turned out to see this most unusual sight. Everyone seemed to be talking at once and pointing fingers in their direction, some even daring to come close enough to touch them, to make sure they were real.

The girls realized the futility of getting a lift in this situation, so they began walking to the outskirts of the village. At a safe distance from their admirers, some of whom had followed them part of the way, they set down their duffel bags and rested in the shade of a poplar tree. Only a few scattered red-roofed barns and browsing cows dotted the farmlands bordering the road. Very little traffic it seemed used this way, so they prepared for a long wait, munching on peaches from orchards along the way.

The quietness of the countryside was disturbed by the tramping of heavy footsteps approaching the spot where Joey and Amy now sat. Looking up, the girls saw two men burdened down by heavy packs and recognized them to be fellow hitch-hikers. The newcomers paused as they reached the girls.

'Had any luck with rides so far, and where are you headed?' the men queried.

'It's been easy, and everyone in Europe has been kind and helpful, and we're off to Pisa.'

'We are too. Bet we get there first.'

'You're on,' challenged the girls as the men continued their trudge down the road.

Four hours elapsed before a car's engine was heard in the distance. Joey and Amy sprang to their feet and grabbed their duffel bags in readiness for the kill. They were desperate by now and would have taken anything that moved. Stepping boldly forward, Amy raised her thumb to the oncoming vehicle—too late to notice that two men occupied the front seat. The car, an old Fiat, came to an abrupt halt, and instantly one young bearded man jumped out to greet them, asking their destination. Yes, they too were headed for Pisa, and he proffered a helping hand to Amy, guiding her to the front seat, next to an older clean-shaven man, while Joey was ushered into the back, he taking up a position next to her.

They passed a mile or two, chatting amiably enough in pidgin English, overtaking as they did so the other two hitch-hikers, who were riding atop a hay wagon!

'See you in Pisa,' yelled Amy through the window.

They waved back in recognition and then were gone from sight.

Joey by now was beginning to feel very uncomfortable. The man next to her had begun to close the gap between them and his hands fumbled for her knees. She inched away as far as she could, but this proved to be no deterrent, for he kept on coming, getting bolder with each move. The driver, too, had become less intent on the road and more interested in the girl at his side. He drove now with one hand only, grasping at Amy with the other.

Speaking as rapidly as possible, so as to be unintelligible to the Italians, Joey and Amy decided to jump from the car as it slowed down on its ascent of the next hill. As the car spluttered and came to a near standstill on a steep incline, the girls threw open their doors and leaped out, running for safety in the direction of a small cafe nearby.

The proprietor stood at the doorway, watching in amazement as the girls fled the two men, now pursuing them. Finally caught, a scuffle followed, words were exchanged, and the disgusted men, muttering to themselves, retreated to their car and went on their way. The girls, shaken by the experience, were close to tears and looked toward the cafe owner for sympathy. He was by now grinning from ear to ear and, with a click of his heels, turned his back on them and disappeared inside.

With disconsolate faces, they wished themselves back to the safety of their digs in London and they swore more prudence in the future if they were to come through unscathed, as each now realised their vulnerability.

Finally they hailed a car driven by a middle-aged businessman. Here at last they felt they would not be molested. He was going to Pisa, and they would be set down on the youth hostel's doorstep.

They reached the outskirts of Pisa at 8:00 p.m., and the driver offered to take them to dinner. As they were by now starving, having had nothing all day but peaches, they gratefully accepted the invitation. They ate till their sides fair burst, were serenaded by the restaurant's strolling musicians, and chatted with their host, who promised to personally take them over Pisa the next day.

On their arrival at the hostel, they were greeted triumphantly by the hitch- hikers whom they had met earlier in the day. After all, they had won the flippant bet!

Having made such an effort to reach this city, both felt pangs of disappointment when they discovered the Leaning Tower was the only noteworthy attraction in the area. Needless to say, they did not have an escorted tour and were glad when the time came to be on their way again.

Headed for the Italian and French Rivieras, the girls were confronted with finding space at the many hostels scattered along the rocky shores of this paradise. Everyone it seemed shared their enthusiasm for spending the balmy nights on the brink of the Mediterranean. They were turned away from several before they finally came across one that, full though it was, permitted the hardy to sleep within the protection of its walls en plein air beneath the stars and, for the more fortunate, to pitch their tents.

Eating at the hostel's cafeteria, Joey and Amy satisfied their hunger first, then went out into the night to stake their claim on a piece of ground that was to serve as their bed. People were sitting or lying around wherever the eye could see, some strumming quietly on guitars, others chewing ravenously on bread, which was to do for their evening meal.

Two young Germans pitched their tent close to where Joey and Amy were squatted. Soon they came over to talk and, seeing the plight of the two girls, offered them protection from the night air within their tent. After their experiences of the previous day still too fresh in their minds, they declined the offer graciously.

Silence fell upon the compound as the weary travellers went to sleep, disturbed only by the waves lapping on the shore and the distant hoot of an owl.

Around midnight, Joey and Amy were woken by the German youths, who insisted they sleep in the tent for the remainder of the night, while they take up a vigil outside. Sensing this to be a sincere gesture of concern for their welfare, the girls put up no objections. On waking with the dawn, they peeked from the tent to find their sentinels curled up and still sound asleep.

Breathtaking in its beauty, the French Riviera lay before them. The hillsides dotted with the red-tiled roofs of splendid villas, each commanding a panoramic view across the wind-teased seas. The fishing boats now lying idle at their moorings under the blazing noontime sun. All was quiet and peace, save for the cicadas droning from aloft in the tall trees, for the French had taken to their beds after a satisfying repast. Only the foreign- born, the ignorant, crazed, or uncivilized roamed abroad. Even the animals had sought shelter from the heat; tails curled around their bodies, eyes drooped in drowsiness, bodies stirring only in rhythm to their breathing. Joey saw it all and yearned to remain longer in this corner of the world, where she had not yet met a rival for its loveliness.

Spain with its Costa Brava and endless stretches of white sandy beaches beckoned invitingly. Pity though, this car in which Amy and Joey were being transported sped along with great urgency. The driver did not give so much as a second glance at the striking landscape, dashing any hopes the girls had harboured for a tour of this region.

Before Joey and Amy realised it, they had arrived in the lovely city of Barcelona. Pointedly they made their way to the stadium, as everyone else in town was doing at that hour, it being nearly 6:00 p.m. The time of the bullfight was at hand, and people en masse were pushing and shoving at the arena's entrance to obtain tickets for this spectacle.

The fortunate ones who had arrived early would get the best and most expensive seats, those in the shade. Others, like Joey and Amy, who could only afford the cheapest, and those who came late, would have to endure the show through squinted eyes.

The splendour of the bullfighters, strutting like peacocks around the battleground, drew gasps of admiration from the stands. Then quite without warning, a hush fell over the crowd as a gate was opened and a bewildered bull made its entrance.

From this moment on, Joey and Amy felt sick to their stomachs as they watched through half-closed eyes the scenes of horror that constituted this sport. The animal was never given a chance from the beginning. He was taunted with capes, poked and jabbed with spear-like weapons and picks, until blood was drawn. He then quickly tired, and foam frothed from his mouth. When he was barely able to stand anymore, the matador, the hero of this deadly game, moved in and finished him off with a thrust of his sword. The crowd went wild with excitement if the beast was killed in one fell swoop of the blade, drawing from them shouts of 'OLE! OLE!'

The matador proceeded next to cut the ear from the animal, proudly displaying it to the audience, before finally flinging it among them. In return for the spectacle of a clean kill, the frenzied mob showed their appreciation by tossing flowers at his feet. To end this tragedy, a team of horses was brought into the ring to drag out the bull's still-warm carcass. Once out of view, the waiting local abattoir would claim the prize.

The two girls also heard about the grace and beauty of the flamenco dancers, who made this city famous. They were unprepared, however, when later that evening in a night club, they watched enthralled at the display of enthusiasm by the onlookers. These enthusiasts all but got up and danced themselves, as the heels of the professionals tapped rhythmically and their castanets clicked with each measured gesture. The colourful costumes too enhanced these dark-haired performers by complementing their dramatic movements. Certainly a sight of beauty after the gory massacre they had witnessed earlier in the day.

Leaving Spain behind, they headed this time for Paris, courtesy of a long- distance truck driver. It was dusk when they arrived in this historic city, and they hoped for a comfortable bed in which to rest.

Hunting high and low for their hostel of the night, they eventually found it, buried beneath the city's streets. Apparently it had once served as public rest rooms, now converted to give shelter to the out-of-pocket traveller.

They spent a few days in Paris, and the first place of interest was the Eiffel Tower.

'Let's walk up, Amy, I want to feel the thrill of it all because you can see through the girders and observe everything below you.'

'What a scary thought! Heights don't agree with me, I'd get vertigo.' 'Really, you never mentioned that before! Will it help if I hold your hand?'

'Sweet of you, Joey, but I'll take the lift and meet you at the top.'

Huffing and puffing, Joey reached the pinnacle to find Amy clinging to the rail on the viewing deck.

'How goes it, Amy?'

'Not bad if I don't look straight down.'

Jumping up and down excitedly, Joey exclaimed, 'Look! We can see all of Paris, well nearly all from here. It's beautiful, and look at all the historic buildings.'

'Hmph, and to think we have old buildings back home,' Amy remarked.

Next stop for the girls was the view from the Arc de Triomphe with the splendid, fashionable, bustling Champs-Élysées at their feet, and the never- ending chaos of traffic horns blaring, as tourists competed with locals to exit this merry-go-round that circled the arc.

'You see that white Renault, Joey? Look, I swear I've seen that poor bloke go round a couple of times.'

'You mean he can't get out of this mess?'

'That or he doesn't know where he's going. Road rules don't seem to exist here!'

'I'm beginning to choke on all the fumes, Amy. Let's go window- shopping on the Boulevarde and perhaps we could indulge ourselves in a cup of coffee at one of those swanky street cafes.'

'I'm with you, girl. Hidden from the sun under those colourful umbrellas will not only be a photo opportunity, but we can people watch as well!'

'Great idea, let's go.'

The next place of interest for the girls was the Louvre, and after a long wait in queues, they headed straight for the Mona Lisa.

'Joey, copies don't do this justice, do they?'

'No, you're so right. The brush strokes and colours come alive in the original.'

They finished their day having seen only a small part of this wonderful museum, but while in Paris, they had also seen the Folies Bergère, which made them giggle, had a picnic by the Seine, knelt respectfully in Notre Dame Cathedral, and tried frogs' legs for the first and last time!

They were now anxious to be back on English soil. They were tired from their long journey and thought of the luxuries of hot baths and comfortable beds.

The White Cliffs of Dover were a welcome sight to Joey and Amy as they approached English shores in their channel ferry. However, London was still a distance off, and because they were now almost broke, they knew the last leg would have to be hitched too.

Braving the road for what they hoped would be the last time, they were soon picked up by a kindly Englishman. Oh, what joy to be able to communicate so easily in their own tongue again! Learning of their financial plight, and not going all the way to London himself, he set them down at a railway station, pressing into their hands as he did so sufficient money to get them home.

Once safely aboard their London-bound train, the two girls were able to reflect on their travels. The beauty, diversity, and narrow escapes, but above all, the human kindness that total strangers had shown them.

Chapter 10

Shivering weather heralded in December, but wedding bells were soon to dispel the cheerlessness of the winter days. Amy and Bob had set the date of the twelfth for tying the knot. Their honeymoon would be the journey home to Australia via the United States and South Pacific, leaving on the thirteenth from Southampton.

Since their return to England after their hitchhiking vacation, Joey and Amy had seen Mary, Joan, and Jim depart for home. It seemed incredible to believe that a year had almost gone by since they'd met. Now they were gone, and soon Amy and Bob would follow. Bob had been determined he would not let Amy out of his sight for so long again. He had missed her terribly, and there was no mistaking the joy and contentment both felt back in each other's company.

The holiday to Europe had done Amy a lot of good, for she was able to think more objectively about her feelings for Bob. It was while away from him that she realised the deep love in her heart and the knowledge that he would always be with her. She appreciated and saw his qualities more plainly than ever before. This was really belonging; this was the security she had yearned for all her life. Running was no longer necessary; her restlessness had been stilled by the man she loved.

It was then with love, and certainty of the future, that Amy had accepted Bob's proposal of marriage. The wedding would be a small quiet affair, performed by a Justice of the Peace, with Joey doing the honours as their main witness.

Joey was as happy about the impending union as the couple themselves. She had watched with great interest the changes that had taken place in Amy. Never before had she seen her so relaxed and assured. It was heart- warming too to see her confidence in handling human relationships strengthening daily. She had found her perfect match, and there was no doubt in Joey's mind that her life would be a happy and fulfilling one.

For herself, Joey had been reluctant to book her passage home as her year neared its end. She was haunted over the past months by the beauty of the French Riviera and had an irresistible urge to return there one more time, if only for a vacation. But her greatest desire would be to live and work there for a span of six months, by which time she felt she would be ready to set sail for home.

Browsing the job columns of the *Times* one Sunday, her eyes came upon an interesting ad:

Temporary Vacancy: Teacher of English wanted for French students in Cannes, France.

Start January 1956.

No experience necessary

Allowance -4- food and board

Reply: Box 2X22. Times.

Elated by this find, Joey immediately wrote a reply.

This was exactly what she had hoped for, and now she prayed she would get the job.

Several days passed before she received an answer and it was with trembling hand that she managed to open the letter. The contents called for an interview in London with a representative from the school to be held in a week's time at a hotel. She had not been rejected, then she still stood a chance of being accepted!

Feeling quite nervous at the prospect of this interview, Joey arrived half an hour earlier than requested. She went straight to the hotel's cafeteria for a cup of tea to help quieten her nerves. Then precisely on time, she took the elevator to the designated floor, walked to the room appointed for the interview, and rapped lightly on the door.

'Come in,' a female voice replied.

On entering, Joey made herself known. 'I'm Joey McPhally. I had an appointment with a Miss Walters at 4:00 p.m.'

'I'm Miss Walters, won't you please sit down,' she said in a friendly tone.

Miss Walters was a young Englishwoman in her late twenties who soon had Joey feeling relaxed.

'Well, Miss McPhally, what incentive did you have for answering our ad?'

'To be quite frank, I fell in love with the Riviera on a recent visit there and longed to return. Your ad gave me the hope to fulfil my wish.'

'Hmm... I assume you've never taught English as a foreign language before?'

'That's right.'

'The course is mainly in English conversation with students ranging in age from 11 to 18. Do you think you'd enjoy work of this kind?'

'I don't know', replied Joey honestly, 'but it would be a challenge and I'd be grateful for the opportunity to try.'

'Do you speak any French?' 'Very little,' confessed Joey.

'Don't apologize, so much the better, for the children will learn more quickly from you if you don't,' added Miss Walters. 'You do realise the pay is small, but then you get your room and board. The school also provides a round-trip train ticket.'

'Sounds perfect,' said Joey, smiling.

'Are there any questions you'd like to ask?'

'Yes', said Joey, 'what kind of school is it, and what's the principal like?'

'It's a French private school, very much like those here in England owned and administered by a wealthy Frenchwoman named Madame Girot. She's married with three children. Very personable lady, or at least I got along well with her and the family when I was there.'

'You mean you don't work there anymore?'

'Good heavens no, I left about four years ago. I'm just acting as a liaison officer for Madame Girot as she was unable to make the trip to England to do the interviewing herself.'

'Why did the previous teacher leave?'

'Pregnancy, and as she was English, she decided to come back home to have her baby. Her husband's working in Cannes, so she'll be returning to France after the birth. By the way, that's the reason for a six-month contract. She hopes to be back to her old job in September.'

'Oh, I see,' said Joey. 'Did you enjoy your work there?'

'Loved it,' came Miss Walter's quick reply. 'I would have stayed on indefinitely, but my mother became ill, forcing my return to London.'

'I'm so sorry, Miss Walters, but if I may, one more question. What are the arrangements regarding food and board?'

'The English teacher will be lodged in a private house not far from Madame Girot, where a small room has been rented. As to meals, you eat breakfast and dinner with the Girot family, and of course, a hot midday meal is provided at the school.'

'The arrangements sound fine to me,' said Joey.

'I must say', broke in Miss Walters after a moment's silence, 'you've impressed me as the kind of girl who would fit in very nicely with the Gir

ot family. You also seem to be sensible and level-headed. Now you do understand that I have others to interview, but I'll let you know my decision in a week?'

'Yes, of course, that'll be fine.'

'I do hope we'll have the pleasure of meeting again.'

'Thank you,' Joey responded as she disappeared, fingers crossed, through the door way.

The wedding day had arrived! The sun poked its head intermittently through the clouds in gesture of blessing for the happy couple. Amy looked radiant in a simple cream-coloured velvet dress adorned with a tiny spray of yellow rosebuds and baby's breath. At her side was a composed but smiling Bob. Joey was the only one who seemed to have the jitters that day.

The ceremony proceeded at an all too rapid rate, and before she knew it, Joey was signing her name as witness to this event.

Amy had been a very dear friend, and now she was about to leave. Joey knew life without her would be less sunshiny and a lot lonelier. She had in a way replaced Joey's family. Always there at the right times to lend a sympathetic ear and a person in whom Joey could trust and confide in completely.

Of course, as a friend, Joey was more than happy that Amy and Bob were married in spite of the fact she was losing her. Amy had managed at last to put her defences down, instead placing her trust in Bob.

A big step for her, but one that finally rid her of doubts and fear concerning enduring relationships. A love like theirs was truly beautiful, and Joey dreamed of the time some man would treat her with the same kind of affection that Bob so openly demonstrated to his bride.

The time of departure from her dear friends suddenly caught up. Joey stood on the dock, tears glistening in the corners of her eyes as she looked up through a misty haze to catch a last glimpse of Amy and Bob leaning far over the rail, waving frantically and throwing airborne kisses to her in farewell. Parting, surely, was to die a little?

She felt forlorn and saddened when she returned to her bedsitter, wanting to be by herself. On entering, she found mail on the floor, which the landlady had pushed under the door. Carelessly flipping through it, she was surprised to find a letter from Miss Walters, for a week had not yet passed. Carefully she opened it, afraid of what she might find, and read the following:

Lycee de Cannes,
18 Rue de Mazargue,
Cannes,
France 13/12/55

Dear Miss McPhally,

It gives me pleasure, on behalf of Madame Girot, to inform you that you are nominated as a teacher of the Lycee de Cannes as of January 21st, 1956. I enclose herewith a letter of employment in duplicate, one of which should be signed by you and returned to me.
I shall contact you at a later date to discuss details of your future work.

Yours Sincerely,
Miss Walters.

Ecstatic, Joey rushed to share the news with her family.

Chapter 11

The best welcome awaiting Joey on her arrival in Cannes had been the warm sunshine and clear skies. Funny how she had almost forgotten the sun's deep penetrating powers, giving a sense of well-being and good health. She sat on the promenade face upturned, greedily drinking in its rays, afraid lest it slip behind a cloud and be gone from her forever.

She had succumbed to its healing warmth, toning the tired and aching muscles left from months of exposure to cold and dampness. In fact, she had to acclimatize all over again!

Joey had found everything as Miss Walters had told her it would be. The Girot family were charming enough, although it was difficult to determine to what degree, as they spoke even less English than she had anticipated, leaving a rather wide communication gap.

Madame Girot was a heftily built middle-aged woman and a person, or so it seemed to Joey, prone to many inexplicable moods. The rest of the family consisted of Monsieur Girot, a man of impeccable manners, who ran the family business and kept the customary mistress. Michele, the spoiled 11- year-old daughter; Jacques, their 16-year-old son, the quiet and studious member of the household; and Jean, 19 years old and away at a military academy. Last but not least was the venerable grand-père, aged 90, deaf, cantankerous, but still with an eye for a pretty woman!

The school housed two hundred students and eight full-time and four part-time teachers. Joey's daily schedule was a rigid one; each lesson of one hour's duration, three in the morning from 8:30 to 11:30 a.m., lunch break until two, and three lessons in the afternoon from 2:00 p.m. to 5:00 p.m. She worked Saturday mornings, but had Thursdays off. She did not like her hours or how the day was divided up, but she enjoyed her students.

On Saturday afternoons, the children often asked her to their 'surprise' parties, which were not surprises in the true sense of the word. She had at first declined, feeling she must keep a safe 'distance' between herself and these pupils in order to maintain discipline and respect in the classroom. She was baffled as to why they would want an 'old' woman like her along anyway. In her own country, this would have been taboo. A teacher there would have dampened the spirits completely! The kids kept begging her to go and finally one Saturday she did. The girls arrived fashionably dressed, some modelling themselves on the Brigitte Bardot look. The boys acted mature for their age, were flirtatious, handsome, and certainly knew how to do the Twist. They insisted in getting Joey on the floor and guided her well through the dance steps while the onlookers clapped their approval. To her utmost surprise, she thoroughly enjoyed herself and they seemed to be doing the same. The students were sophisticated, attentive, and respectful throughout, and everyone agreed they'd had a good time.

On the Monday following the disco, Joey was anxious to see what the attitude in class would be like. Normal, completely normal, was the only way it could be described. Nobody in the class felt their liberties of Saturday could be used to advantage or be allowed to permeate the schoolroom. As a result, Joey was seen more frequently at these affairs and built up an excellent rapport with her students without jeopardizing her position as teacher.

Midday lunches at school turned into marathons. Those who stayed there to eat had two and a half hours of time in which to gorge themselves. Joey had at first thought it was a senseless waste of time, but later agreed that the meals were worth taking the time to savour. Deliciously prepared in the school's kitchen, they were available to teachers and students as a smorgasbord. The choices ran the full gamut of soups, meats, including frogs' legs, seafood, and desserts. The students, especially the boys it seemed, could never get their fill. Red wine was for the adults only and was an excellent beverage after all! One day, not knowing how much liquor she could comfortably hold, Joey became very light-headed. When the afternoon lessons commenced, she was all but tripping the light fantastic!

Joey's lodging was located in a villa at about half a mile from the Girots'. She had her own entrance on ground level, situated behind the garage. You entered it directly from the garden stepping then into a small but pleasantly furnished room. A bookcase ran along one wall over the bed, a hand basin was next to a large oak cupboard, and there was a writing desk with a chair in the corner by the door. On the floor was a beautiful Persian rug. This was the extent of the furnishings, but the room could not have comfortably held more pieces.

Madame Gilbert was the lady of the house and let this one room only as a special favour to Madame Girot. Joey had got the impression from their very first meeting that Madame Gilbert was a no-nonsense woman. She spoke plainly and directly of what she expected of her tenant in order that she might maintain a high degree of respectability among her neighbours. It was therefore made quite clear to Joey that male friends could not call on her no matter what the hour of the day or night, for this would certainly cast suspicions on the integrity of Madame and Monsieur Gilbert. Joey quickly set the lady at ease by assuring her that she would indeed respect her wishes on this matter, as she herself was not the kind of girl to have liaisons of that nature. Both women had been frank and open in their discussion and understood each other reasonably well. Joey had used her room so far for sleeping purposes only, as she spent the greater part of her time at school or with the Girot family. In the eyes of Madame Gilbert, she made the ideal tenant, rarely seen and never heard.

Two months since her arrival in Cannes, Joey had still found no friends of
her own age. She was always it seemed too young or too old, no matter what party or function she attended. Madame and Monsieur Girot had a large circle of friends

and gave many parties, all of which Joey attended dutifully. These people were much older than she was, and often Joey would leave discreetly to avoid the further boredom she felt in their company. The language barrier proved to be as much of a problem as the generation gap. She knew she must adapt temporarily to this situation even though she yearned for companionship from her elusive peers.

Easter had ushered in many carnivals and exciting events to keep Joey fascinated, intrigued, and her mind off her growing loneliness; for the likes of these she had never seen before! The streets were strewn with flower petals and parades were constantly afoot. With the carnivals had appeared a new breed of man, one that seemed born in the wake of so much colour and festivity. The artists and musicians from colder northern climes had come to capture the imagination and rouse the souls of the fun-seeking tourists and the natives of Cannes. These days the promenades were alive with artists, and the sidewalk cafes reverberated with the sounds of strumming guitars made by these wandering minstrels.

It was not a new sight to the residents of Cannes for every year around Easter saw their return. They were mainly young people with talent, who sought a paradise in which to express their creativity, and in turn market their gifts, enabling them perhaps to return to college for another year. They asked for little, but gave much, and were welcomed by the locals because of their ability to lure the tourists into their houses of business.

Joey found herself seated at one such cafe on a Saturday afternoon in March. She had been busy shopping and now was relaxed, sipping a long cool drink. The sun was particularly strong for that time of year, but a pleasant onshore breeze cooled her.

She was idly watching the constant parade of people pass and re-pass on the promenade. In fact, this had become quite a hobby of hers, getting more fascinating each time she indulged in it. She fancied herself almost an expert by now in distinguishing different nationalities by way of their dress and manners.

So absorbed had Joey been in this game of hers that she failed to hear or notice the two young men now entertaining the patrons of this cafe.

They sang folk and popular music to the accompaniment of their guitars. Their repertoire finally exhausted, they moved among the tables collecting what they could from their audience.

Joey became conscious of eyes gazing at her and turned quickly to come face-to-face with one of the musicians who was standing beside her table holding out a grubby, man-sized handkerchief for a tip no matter how small. He was tall, blond, and she thought very Nordic-looking, judging at the same time his age to be about 29. A little older than the usual crowd that played at these restaurants, certainly he was no student, and she wondered what had brought him to Cannes to lead this insecure type of existence, more often associated with the very young.

Fumbling in her purse for some change, she found to her embarrassment that she had none, and certainly she couldn't afford to give a note. She looked up in a flustered manner and said apologetically, 'I'm sorry I don't have any change, but if you'll come back when I've paid for my drink, I'll be glad to give you something.'

He, smiling, replied in fluent English, 'Never mind, however, I could do with a drink, and I'd be glad to buy you another if I'm permitted to sit down.'

Without waiting for Joey's reply, he had slipped into a seat beside her and snapped his fingers at the waiter for service, giving little opportunity for her to refuse his offer.

They talked at first of superficial matters, as strangers are apt to do, before they felt comfortable enough in each other's company to direct the conversation to a more personal level.

Joey learned that he was Swedish, from Stockholm, and that his name was Jan Eckberg. For several years, he told her, he and his friend had escaped the severe winters of the North to come to the warm South.

They too had been hypnotized by the Riviera on their first visit and had been drawn back year after year. Both men abhorred the usual nine-to-five workday, but tolerated it during the winter months so they could have this life of relative freedom for the remaining part of the year.

From Joey, he found out her reasons for staying in Cannes, also her nationality, name, and the location of her school, which were all revealed during the course of the conversation.

Glancing suddenly at her watch, Joey was surprised and a little concerned at the lateness of the hour, for she had promised to assist Madame Girot with the decorations for her party that evening. Jumping to her feet, she hurriedly thanked Jan for the drink and pleasant talk and was headed in the direction of a bus, leaving him open-mouthed with surprise.

20 March 1956

Dear Diary,

What an interesting man I met today. Very talented and suave, I must say! I wonder will he contact me? Will he? Won't he? I'd like him to. I'm going to remember him anyway by the following poem:

J. McP.

Wand'ring Minstrel

Just a wand'ring minstrel man was he,
In tattered coat and scarf of red hue,
Making merry music hither and yon,
To each man he perchanced to espy.
Guitar slung on shoulder in rakish style,

And a provocative gleam in eye,
He wooed and entranced his listeners each one,
till the sun set in a rose red sky.
Then with a wink and nod of the head,
He passed his 'kerchief among his friends,
In hope of getting a penny or two,
To pay for a good hot bowl of soup.
Sometimes our minstrel was down on his luck,
But on the whole he fared pretty well,
Contented and happy the live-long day,
To play his music with joy and love.
You may glimpse him sometime along the way,
Playing ballads unfettered and free,
Spreading gladness to his listeners each one
For nothing more than the price of a meal.

J. McP.

Chapter 12

Joey was preparing to leave school the following Monday afternoon when the secretary said a young man was waiting for her in the library.

A little annoyed at being detained, she strode in to find out who could be wanting to talk with her at this late hour. The last person she expected to see when she entered was Jan Eckberg, who was standing in readiness to greet her. She suddenly felt glad he had come, and her face lit up with pleasure as she walked towards him.

'Surprised to see me?' he said, smiling.

'Am I ever! How in the world did you remember where I worked?'

'I've a pretty good memory for some things,' he teased. 'Just as well too, because the way you ran off the other day didn't leave too many hopes for further meetings, did it?'

'I'm really sorry about that, I hope you didn't think me rude, but I did have a prior commitment.'

'No harm done, I found you again,' he said with twinkling eyes. 'Actually I came to ask a favour of you.'

'Oh, I thought there must be some catch, what is it?' asked Joey.

'I wondered if you'd do some babysitting tonight?'

'Babysitting! Have you a tribe of kids stashed away somewhere?'

'Of course not', he laughed, 'it's for a friend of mine and I promise I'll make it up to you if you'll help us out.'

'But I don't know them, and what about the child, a boy or girl? How would he or she like to be left with a stranger? And I know nothing about babies.'

'Relax, Joey, he's 5 years old. Inger will have him in bed before we leave, so don't worry.'

'Well, I really don't mind as long as it's only temporary and it's not too late. After all, I have to work tomorrow.'

'We'll be back around midnight and then I'll see you home,' Jan assured her. 'Can you come now?'

'Now? But I'm expected for dinner at Madame Girot's.'

'You're invited to eat with us if you like. Look, why not tell Madame Girot that you'll be eating out?'

'Well, will you wait here a few minutes while I find her?'

'Take your time,' said Jan, picking up a magazine.

Joey was back in no time at all to inform Jan that she had straightened out matters with Madame Girot and was ready to leave as soon as she changed.

'That's great, and thanks for being so helpful. We were in a fix and I don't know how we'd have managed without you,' he said sincerely.

In a wink, she returned.

'Come on, let's go,' said Jan.

As he spoke, Joey scrutinised this very attractive man perhaps for the first time. Not only could he speak English grammatically like a native, but had five other languages: Swedish, German, Dutch, French, and Italian, which he knew equally well. Standing at least six feet tall, slim, and broad- shouldered and a face set off by mischievous blue eyes, a crown of short blond curls, coiffed one imagined by running fingers through them, and a very full-lipped kissable mouth. Gorgeous! A man who could have any woman he wanted. How lucky, Joey thought, to be singled out by him, but why?

He conducted her through the narrow back streets into the old section of Cannes, which was much quainter and had a more authentic French air than the newer part of town that bordered the sea, where the tourists mainly congregated.

Finally, they came to an old crumbling apartment building and entered the lobby through an ornately carved wooden door with a very heavy wrought iron door handle. Rusted metal, overstuffed letter boxes with names, and unit numbers of the residents lined the damp peeling-painted walls. Jan led Joey by the hand up the unlit, winding, in-need-of-repair, stone staircase to the fourth floor, and knocked on Stig and Ingrid's door.

They were ushered into a small, but attractively decorated apartment, where the odours of cooking made Joey think of home. She was introduced to Jan's musical partner, Stig Anderson, a short frail-looking man with twinkling eyes and the woman he lived with, Ingrid Engeliau, a slim attractive blonde with a welcoming smile.

Ingrid had taken part-time work as a waitress in a local restaurant, as the small pittance Stig brought home from guitar playing was certainly nowhere near enough money to keep three people fed. She had a good arrangement with a neighbour who babysat for her evenings, and then in return, she looked after the other woman's children during the day. This had proved to be most satisfactory until the neighbour came down with flu. Ingrid was grateful for Joey's willingness to help out and offered to pay her for her services.

Joey refused any money and said she'd be glad to continue babysitting for her until the neighbour was fully recovered.

With young Hans tucked safely in bed, Ingrid, Stig, and Jan bid Joey farewell and went off to their respective work. Joey availed herself of the many magazines scattered about the living room and settled comfortably for an evening of relaxation.

At about eleven thirty, she heard voices and footsteps on the staircase outside and was happy to know her friends had already returned. They seemed quite elated when they entered the apartment, and Joey soon discovered the reason for their joy. Jan and Stig had a particularly successful evening, for the restaurants in which they'd played had more than a fair share of generous patrons. Spreading out the now familiar handkerchiefs on the kitchen table, the two prepared to divide their takings.

Seeing Joey's surprised expression at the obvious pleasure they derived from counting out their spoils, they explained to her that living from hand to mouth as they did, this night had made them feel like millionaires. Of course, she could not fully understand nor appreciate their emotions, as she had never put herself in a position of total dependence on other's charity in order to stay alive. She could see, though, what a precarious position they were in and was happy for their sakes that they would not starve, at least not for a while anyway.

Joey was now eager to be on her way home, for it was getting late and she knew how poorly her performance at school would be if she were tired and irritable for want of sleep. Taking her leave of Ingrid and Stig and promising them she would return the next evening, as young Hans had given her no trouble, she hurried out into the night with Jan at her heels.

It was a beautiful warm evening, one for enjoying, and it suddenly occurred to Joey what an utter waste it was to have to sleep away the magical hours it still had to offer. The moon was full and high in the heavens, playing hide-and-seek behind the clouds, so that in a moment, one's face was clearly lit by its beams, the next mysteriously shrouded in its shadows.

They were walking along the waterfront, for the buses had stopped running at midnight, when Jan interrupted Joey's reverie.

'I know a shortcut to where you live,' he suddenly announced.

'You do! Where is it?'

'You see that next bluff?' he asked, indicating it with his finger. 'There's a small stone pathway at the foot of the rocks that winds around by the sea and will save us having to climb the hills via the roadway.'

'Yes, but where does it come out?'

'Near the bottom of your street,' Jan replied.

'You're sure about that—I don't want to get lost?'

'Of course I'm sure, I know this area pretty well.'

Taking Joey by the hand and squeezing it reassuringly, he guided her down to the small path.

'Thank goodness I changed into my pedal pushers and sandals or I might not have got down so easily.'

'I'm always in shorts and sandals. I guess you'd call them my "uniform". No reason for me to get all dressed up now, is it?' Jan said smugly.

Apparently this route served not only as a shortcut, but as a sort of pedestrian scenic way, and a thoroughfare to enable bathers to enter the water directly from the rocky ledges. In fact, Joey could see in the moonlight how the beautiful small inlets were secluded between the rocks. How much better for swimming and sunbathing it would be here, away from the overcrowded public beaches. These small coves were completely hidden from the roadway, and the privacy one would get by bathing here seemed in itself worthwhile.

The two, still hand in hand, continued along the narrow path, Joey every so often letting out squeals of delight as the waves crashed on the rocks spewing spray all over her, while she instinctively pressed closer to Jan for protection. He immediately took advantage of her closeness to encircle her in his arms and kiss her passionately. She responded warmly to his embrace, her body trembling from his caresses. Reluctantly he relaxed his hold on her and sat down on a nearby rock. He pulled a pack of Gauloise cigarettes from his pocket and offered one to Joey, who declined with the shake of her head.

'Come and sit beside me,' he invited. She obediently moved to his side and sat down. He put his arm around her and puffed on his cigarette. They said nothing, each with their own thoughts, both staring at the sea and listening to the waves beating on the outcrops of rock. Joey finally broke what had seemed to be an interminable silence between them.

'I'd like a puff on your cigarette after all,' she said shyly.

He gave her the one he had been smoking; gingerly she put it to her lips and took a long draw on it. To her embarrassment, she almost choked to death coughing and spluttering in a most unladylike manner. In disgust, she tossed the butt into the sea.

'Oh, horrible', she groaned, 'why didn't you warn me?'

'I thought it best you find out for yourself,' he said, laughing.

'Never again, I swear,' said Joey.

'Wise girl, better not to start,' Jan added, springing to his feet. 'Come on, Joey,' he said, offering his hands to help her up.

They arrived at her gate, arms around each other, hair hanging dank from the sea-spray, both feeling slightly intoxicated by the presence of the other. Joey, who normally acted rationally, could not explain her total disregard for the time, the opinions her neighbours may be forming of her at that very moment, while watching in disbelief through cracks in their shutters, nor the consequences she must face for this night of sheer joy. She managed for the first time in her life to free herself to enjoy his company for the short time they were together.

The clock in the church tower chimed the hour of 4:00 a.m. She must go in to bed for she had to be at school in four and a half hours' time and didn't know how she'd make it.

Finally convincing Jan of her necessity to get some rest, they kissed and she then entered the garden and stealthily crossed it to reach the safety of her room. In bed at last, she tossed and turned for her mind and body were still very much alert. It was unbelievable that she had allowed this stranger so readily into her life. Her parents would never have approved. Certainly Joey had never before allowed anyone else to mesmerise her. So why now? At that moment, she discerned that in all probability, any demands Jan made of her in the future would be most difficult to refuse. He held some indefinable power over her, which was frightening in its intensity.

At 7:00 a.m., she left her bed to face the day. Strangely enough, she felt no weariness, only an inner excitement at the prospect of seeing Jan again that evening.

Chapter 13

Joey had been given the option to renew her contract for another school year if she wished, as the teacher on maternity leave had decided to remain in England indefinitely. Of course Joey was overjoyed at the prospect of remaining in Cannes another year, especially as her relationship with Jan had developed. She soon informed Madame Girot that she would be more than delighted to stay on, but when she wrote to her family later about the decision, she felt selfish in her justifications for prolonging the stay. She quickly brushed these feelings aside, however, as soon as the letter had been mailed.

In late May, Joey returned from school one afternoon and was at first astonished and then angered to find Jan, sitting casually on her bed reading a paper. She was struck temporarily speechless, while Jan looked up at her smiling.

'Hello, darling, did you have a good day?'

'What are you doing here?' she finally blurted out. 'You know I've told you I can't have male visitors in this room. I thought you understood my position and respected it. How will I be able to explain this to Madame Gilbert?'

Tears smarted her eyes while she spoke, as she realized the problems that could arise from this thoughtless act of Jan's. Her reputation sullied and her standing with the Girot family put in jeopardy if Madame Gilbert chose to inform her employer of this violation of trust. Her job and chances of remaining in Cannes seemed suddenly threatened, and she was furious with Jan for putting her in this situation.

'Jan, how could you do this to me? I promised Madame Gilbert I'd comply with her wishes and you've prevented me from doing just that,' she cried. 'I don't know how I'll ever be able to look her in the face again.'

Jan rose from the bed and moved to where Joey was still glued to the spot and put his arms lovingly around her.

'But, darling, if you'll give me a chance, I'll explain everything to you.'

'What's there to explain?' replied Joey angrily. 'You're here, aren't you, and that doesn't need any clarification.'

'Hold it', retorted Jan impatiently, 'how do you think I got in here without a key?'

'I hadn't thought of that. How did you?'

'That's exactly what I wanted to explain. Now if you've calmed down enough to let me continue, maybe you'll understand that everything's perfectly legitimate and you need fear no reprisal from Madame Gilbert. It's all very simple,' he continued. 'I approached her this afternoon, explained who I was and that we were serious. In fact we had quite a long chat. She understood and sympathized with my position and finally gave me a duplicate gate key, and here I am.'

'Just as simple as that,' said Joey with disbelief. 'I don't understand the woman at all if what you say is true. How could she change her mind so suddenly about this?'

'That's the whole point, darling, she hasn't changed her mind at all. You just don't understand the French very well.'

'Are you telling me that she didn't mean what she said concerning male visitors?' queried a perplexed Joey.

'Oh, she meant that, all right, but while she won't tolerate a number of different male visitors, she does understand and will accept one special friend, as long as she's assured the affair is a serious one.'

'Really!' said Joey nonplussed.

'Different nationalities, different standards, and now you're living in France, Joey, and must understand the French mentality and their interpretation of your actions. So you see, you have nothing to be afraid of. I'm here with Madame Gilbert's blessing and intend to stay as long as you'll have me,' Jan concluded.

'You must be out of your mind', said Joey disbelievingly, 'you mean you actually intend to move in and live with me, like man and wife?'

'Of course, darling, why do you sound so shocked? I thought you'd be as happy as I am. After all, when two people are in love, what is more natural than to be with one another all the time?'

'It's just that I never expected to find myself in a position of this kind. I've always been old-fashioned enough to believe that when two people loved each other, they married, and that was that,' exclaimed Joey innocently. 'Besides I don't think I could reconcile myself to any other way of living.'

'That's really a very Victorian way of thinking.' Jan smiled. 'I thought you loved me and you'd want to be with me too.'

'You know I love you, Jan, and that you're the real reason for my staying on in Cannes.'

'Well then, I can't see any reason for us not being together as much as possible. I want to be a part of you, to share everything. I feel alone when you're not with me. You give me strength and comfort, and God knows I can't be parted from you anymore,' Jan said with deep emotion in his voice.

Joey felt herself weakening and giving way to this man she loved. In his presence, she was totally defenceless and stripped of any facility to argue against him.

'Well, I guess if Madame Gilbert doesn't object to the arrangement', said Joey, 'everything should be all right, only I'm concerned about Madame Girot's reaction if she finds out. Maybe I'll lose my job.'

'Nonsense, she doesn't need to know, and even assuming she did find out, it's no business of hers how you conduct your private life, providing you do your job well.'

'I guess you're right, Jan,' said Joey resignedly.

Jan, seeing he had won Joey over, now took her in his arms and whispered tenderly, 'Darling, I love you so much, promise you'll never leave me—never?'

'Jan, you know I'll never leave you.'

On an impulse, Jan swept Joey up off her feet and carried her to the bed. She did not fight off his advances, nor the desire she felt for him welling up uncontrollably within her, but gave herself to him, a oneness with the man she loved.

It was dark before they stirred from the comfort of each other's arms to get ready for the evening ahead of them. Jan was going with Stig to play guitar, while Joey dressed for dinner with the Girot family.

Stealing out into the night, they crossed the garden to the gate. Joey's eyes were downcast, her head slightly lowered as she passed beneath the Gilberts' living-room window, afraid still, despite all Jan had said, of unseen fingers pointing accusingly at her and unspoken words mocking and jeering at her promiscuity.

In spite of her sincere feelings, her initiation into womanhood that very evening, she knew she'd not be easily reconciled to this way of life.

For the love of a man, she had gone against her grain and, for this reason, must carry within her a loss of dignity and burden of guilt. Little price really to pay for the intense happiness mutually enjoyed?

Chapter 14

Summer had evaporated, leaving in its aftermath memories of lazy times spent on warm pebbly beaches and invitingly clear waters in whose depths myriads of fish had sought refuge from the ever-present dangers that lurked beneath their surface.

Joey, tanned and healthy-looking after her vacation spent as a 'beachcomber', had returned to work with renewed zeal. With the passing of the months, she had found herself falling into a lifestyle to match that of Jan's. This was no mean task for the schedule she now kept was a rigorous and demanding one. She was up early each morning to perform her duties as a teacher and retiring late at night so she could greet Jan after his late- night stands in the restaurants.

She had liked, even enjoyed the role of waiting for her man's return, no matter how late the hour. She felt the long evenings spent alone were more than compensated for, when finally she would hear his footfall in the garden and his characteristic knock on the door. For then again they would be alone together, to share and reflect upon the events of the evening.

Lately, however, in these wee hours of the morning, lying side by side in the darkness, Jan had begun interrogating Joey. He seemed especially eager to learn about any past romances that she had experienced, and the motivations behind these attachments.

Joey readily responded and truthfully, for she had nothing to hide from him. She'd had a few mild flirtations, but nothing of consequence, and she brushed them aside nonchalantly.

She began to feel uneasy when Jan expressed his dissatisfaction with her replies, for she could not comprehend what he was getting at. She had been honest, what else did he want? He knew she had lost her virginity to him, so why was he trying to make something out of her past that wasn't there?

For his part, Jan insisted that in order to know and understand another person well, past experiences, especially those of old romances and the motivating force behind them, were of paramount importance in helping to unravel the intricacies of the human character and help to predict the trend of one's future behaviour. He expressed his disappointment again, at the same time impressing upon her the seriousness he attached to her answers.

Joey vehemently disagreed with Jan's lines of questioning, admitting that while this might hold true for casual flirtations, and here even there was no certainty, the pattern could be upset drastically with the involvement of deep love. To her, the gathering of skeletons from the cupboard, no matter how innocent, bore no relevance whatsoever to their present or future together. She after all had accepted him for what he was and would continue to place her love and trust in him, until she had good cause not to. That was all she asked of him in return.

Clearly the two could not agree, and Joey knew that if the relationship were to survive, she would have to be the one to try to accommodate his insecurities.

For Joey, the task of recapturing the thoughts and feelings she had experienced with former beaux was not only difficult, but distasteful to her in light of her present involvement with Jan. However, she desperately sifted through the remnants of their memories locked within her mind to analyse the reasons that had prompted her to behave the way she had.

With repeated questioning from Jan to help with her recall, her answers now sounded foolish. Had she really allowed herself to be kissed and cuddled by one, because she had felt indebted to him for giving her an evening out? To another because he was sexy, and a third for his flattery? Yet as well as she could remember, these were the stimuli for her romantic encounters. With disbelief herself at these revelations, she spoke with hesitancy in her voice.

This was Jan's cue to take her up immediately on the honesty of her remarks. Why did she hesitate? Was she ashamed of her own inane reasons for the partial sex acts she had indulged in? Was she the kind of woman who could participate in such deeds without deep feeling or emotion? No matter how honestly she tried to answer his questions, he was never satisfied. To Joey, the most frightening aspect of these inquisitions was the twist he gave to even the most innocent escapades involving men. Her hitch-hiking trip had been made to appear as an excuse for flaunting herself before every available male, while a kiss and embrace became a heavy petting session. He had even likened her to a prostitute, not because of any physical involvement, but due to her attitudes towards her liaisons, which he had deduced were based purely on sex. This he found intolerable in a female.

Joey didn't know if Jan was prompted by over possessiveness, acute jealousy, or madness. He had also begun taking her to task about her mode of dress.

'I don't like you wearing those halter-dress necklines, baring your knees, or using bright red lipstick. Is it to seduce other males? You know it's not for me. I prefer you without make-up at all,' he chastised.

Feeling hurt, Joey whimpered back, 'I just do it for me.' 'For yourself? Why would you do that?'

'Because I like to look nice, makes me feel good.' 'Well, I don't like other men ogling you and that's that!'

While this in itself did not cause Joey undue worry, nor present a definite threat to their association, she did however feel an encroachment upon her self-expression and individuality. She complied only to avoid further friction and argument over a matter she considered trivial.

Joey gradually began to feel like a criminal being subjected to the third degree. She sensed there must be some deeper reason for Jan's obsession with her past. Never satisfied, always hungering for more. With this knowledge, doubts began to crowd her mind.

Was it that he didn't want to believe in her? Or was he so insecure that he needed constant reassurance of her love and absolute fidelity? Maybe he had guilt feelings about his own past philanderings, which by now Joey had discovered were innumerable, and wanted to find or invent a partner of similar shadiness to help justify his own promiscuous behaviour. Or could he be setting the stage for the perfect alibi to opt out when he had grown tired of her?

Until these 'sessions' had begun, Joey had thought of their relationship as almost perfect. They possessed the ability to laugh with each other, rather than at one another, which Joey considered a most important ingredient for happiness. They had taken enormous pleasure in being able on rare occasions to sit sipping wine at a patio cafe, hands entwined, thoughts one, each sensing instinctively the desires of the other.

They had strolled the beach at night talking—yes, they were always talking. Joey had learned from Jan that conversation was more than just relating facts and observations and should be used more frequently as a virile channel through which even the most reserved of people could express their feelings without shame or fear of derision. She had bared her heart to him, which was contrary to the beliefs of her upbringing, releasing it seemed a flow of pent-up emotions, guilt, and hidden fears. She had felt re-invigorated.

Love to Joey was being an integral part of another, to mesh and diffuse one with the other, with ease and naturalness, till finally the two became as one, inseparable, forever secure in the knowledge of the other. She had felt like this with Jan. Then, in remembrance, a smile brushed her lips as she vividly recalled his words soon after their meeting: 'My heart leaped when I met you.' She had understood.

Why then had this cloud appeared in the form of past bogies to endanger the close bond they shared? Or was love in reality different from that of her cherished ideal, with suffering a necessary facet?

Chapter 15

The last days of October saw the departure of even the most reluctant of tourists from this Mediterranean resort. Among them were Stig Anderson, his live-in girlfriend Ingrid Engellau, and her son, Hans.

During the past month, Jan and Stig had been greatly affected financially by the gradual disappearance of the people on whom their very lives depended.
The cafes and restaurants, which had once been so gay with their merrymaking patrons, were now all but deserted. Many were shuttered fast against the cold night air and the brisk breezes, which whipped in off choppy seas. Inside the mood was sombre, save for a few muffled voices and the occasional clink of a glass as it made contact with a marble-topped table.

Even the waterfront had taken on a new image. Once alive with the incessant movement of craft of all shapes and sizes, navigating their way in and out of the harbour, they now lay abandoned by man to idly tug and strain at their moorings with the rise and fall of the sea's swell.

The promenades were ghostly corridors, echoing the footsteps of lonely walkers, while the floodlights served to focus attention upon these phantoms of the night.

Loathe as they were to leave their summer retreat, Stig and Ingrid had decided to return to Sweden in pursuit of work. This time, however, Jan would not accompany them.

He had decided to try his luck in getting a job in Cannes so he could remain with Joey, and she, afraid lest he should leave, assured him of the little financial assistance she could give. At least he had a roof over his head at no extra cost, and simple meals could be had at a nominal price if one knew the restaurant proprietors, as Jan did. He needed little else for survival and decided to stay.

For him it was a great opportunity to remain in the country of his choice and share his life with Joey. He suffered no pangs of guilt on being a 'kept' man. He considered this a temporary state only and clearly showed Joey's love for him in spite of her knowledge about his inability to find the 'perfect' job environment. After all, a natural-enough reaction on her part. Wouldn't he do the same if the position were reversed?

Since completing high school, Jan had drifted in and out of work, with the hope of finding a job that could absorb and interest him. From dishwashing, assembly line, sales, fruit picking, clerical, language interpretation, odd jobs here and there and from country to country. He would stay maybe a week, or perhaps until he felt the monotony of his work and robot-like movements bearing down upon his soul.

Each time he took a job, he became disgusted with himself as well as those around him. How could they so easily resign themselves to this kind of existence where warmth and friendliness, interest and creativity never entered into their daily lives? Money seemed to have been their only inspiration at the cost of any other values they may have had in the past. Jan was not so willing to abandon his ideals altogether, to become another unhappy, disgruntled human being, adding to the already overpopulated ranks of human misery. Of course he realized he must compromise in order to survive unless he took to begging and, therefore, resigned himself to doing some form of work.

Meeting Stig had been fortunate, for they both shared the same ideals, and a natural partnership was formed. They pooled their musical ability and were able to live as 'free' men for at least part of the year, making the time spent at dull inane work, if not an acceptable solution, at least a more bearable one.

This happy association had by now lasted five years, but Jan had doubts for some time as to how long their present lifestyle could persist in the face of the deepening bond and need for each other that Stig and Ingrid felt. They had met two winters before in their native Stockholm, and for the past two summers, Ingrid and Hans had accompanied Jan and Stig to Cannes. Being a mother and the sole guardian of her child, Ingrid was looking more and more to greater stability and security for her son, especially now as he had reached school age. He was a responsibility that she could not disregard in order to follow her own whims and desires, no matter how important they were to her at the time. Her child's needs must be put first. She had made her feelings known to both Stig and Jan and at the same time made it clear that she would not try to come between them by insisting Stig remain with her out of any sense of duty or moral obligation. He was free to make his decision independently and without restraint. She loved Stig and, for this reason, wanted him to be happy with the choice he must make.

Jan and Stig had strongly shared the same philosophy that marriage was too confining for the parties involved to be able to remain individualistic, alive and interesting; for like most work, the deadliness of routine and habit slowly dulls the senses and desires, inspirations and conversations, leaving each partner with a sense of frustration and futility in his respective role. They had observed these traits in their own parents and in too many of their married friends to remain aloof from the scepticism they felt for the married way of life and did not wish to follow or blunder along the same calamitous path as their forefathers.

This philosophy was, of course, completely foreign to Joey, for she was the product of a happy home and parents and had witnessed the marriage of her best friends Amy and Bob, which in her mind had been the perfect culmination of mutual love. She knew from the outset Jan's views on marriage, although she did not fully understand them. They had seemed to her like petty excuses for not wanting to face up to responsibility or commitments. However, she did not argue the case with him, convinced that in time his point of view would change, as she was certain Stig's had. Certainly she would place no demands on him now.

It was a doubtful Jan then who bade leave of his friend Stig. Doubtful because he did not know which choice Stig would make concerning their future as a musical team. He thought he knew him so well, yet even now as the train chugged out of the station, his mind was besieged with unanswerable questions. Had the passage of time dulled Stig's ideals and made him susceptible to society's codes? Could his love of a woman have changed his thinking radically enough for him to contemplate marriage? Jan's uncertainties about their partnership seemed to grow more acute as the ever-quickening train set distance between them. Guitar playing and a life free from problems faded too, as the train disappeared from view round a bend in the track.

Finally with head bowed in contemplation, and hands thrust in pockets, Jan made his way homeward to Joey.

Chapter 16

Finding work was more difficult than Jan had anticipated. Even though he spoke French fluenxtly, dressed in a smart suit, collar, and tie, prospective employers were hesitant to hire him. Not only did he lack a work permit, but his past wanderings and instability gave them little assurance of his reliability in the future. He was met with one rejection after another. Day after day, he faced the same humiliating and degrading interviews, returning home to Joey in the evenings depressed by his lack of success.

To add to their already-decreasing optimism and morale, Joey's worst fears were confirmed when a doctor assured her that she was indeed pregnant. She had scurried from his office, tears stinging her eyes and resentment toward Jan in her heart. Stumbling into a cafe, she had sought out a corner table, slumped into her seat, and ordered a cappuccino, then when the coffee was put in front of her, pushed it away as the smell made her feel nauseous. Joey sincerely hoped she would recover her composure sufficiently enough to return home and break the news to Jan.

Jan received the news with comparative calm when Joey blurted out her story. He assured her not to worry as he knew a prostitute, who was worldly wise, and therefore was sure to be able to help Joey in some way or another! They would visit her, he promised that day.

Joey was horrified, not only because Jan actually knew a prostitute, but the idea of meeting one herself. She had heard numerous stories about them and had surmised they would be hard, unfeeling, and almost inhuman. She shuddered at the thought of coming face-to-face with such a creature, but could see no alternative to Jan's suggestion, on which she now heavily relied. Clearly she would not be able to have this baby. Jan obviously did not want to be saddled with a family, nor was he in any position to provide for her. She, on the other hand, would be dismissed from her job instantly. How could her pregnancy, in light of her circumstances, be explained away to the students and their parents without the school itself feeling shame? Obviously Madame Girot would have to fire her. Then what? She could not turn to her parents for help or sympathy as they were twelve thousand miles away. Nor did she wish to subject them to the humiliation she now felt, nor the unhappiness this news would bring. Without work, she could not provide for her child, and clearly this responsibility lay in her hands alone. It was with these thoughts then that she went along with Jan's wishes.

While threading their way through a seamy part of town, Joey clung to Jan for security, her eyes darting forever back and forth from corner to corner, looking with bewildered amazement as the 'ladies' went about their business. She, of course, had never before observed their techniques in securing a 'trick', nor the way in which the 'prospects' reacted to the overtures, and she found the scene degrading. They seemed to congregate on street corners or dallied half-obscured in dim doorways, but in each and every case, without exception, one was always aware of the clinking of keys, bunches of keys. With the approach of a likely contact, groups dispersed and forms emerged from their caches ready for the 'sell'! Each one appeared to be aware of her territorial rights and daren't step over her boundary for fear of reprisal from the others, which would be severe. Street fights were not uncommon if this unwritten law was violated, with all joining in against the perpetrator, leaving her finally to lick her wounds and seek an uncontested arena. When finally, after ground rules had been followed, the designated prostitute would sidle up to her quarry, with subdued discourse, followed by various hand movements and body language, suggesting to the casual eye that an arrangement was definitely being made. Shortly thereafter, the woman with swinging hip movements would head off in the direction of her abode, heels tapping and keys once more jingling with each step, the contractee in tow some feet behind with downcast head—deal clinched.

'Will you stop staring,' came Jan's sudden reprimand.

'Was I? Oh, I didn't mean to,' apologised Joey. 'I am just so appalled at what's going on.'

'Appalled! At what? Prostitutes going about their business. You'd really think you were born yesterday, Joey. You're still so näive.'

'I guess I am näive', snapped Joey, 'but don't blame me for my upbringing.'

'What kind was that? Some weird type of isolation from reality to make you feel superior? Good girls don't wander into neighbourhoods like this, etc.'

'That's right,' blurted Joey.

'Interesting, considering the reason we're here, or had you forgotten?' quipped Jan. 'You're not such a good girl anymore, you know.'

'If I'm not, then I only have you to thank.'

They walked on in silence, Joey now oblivious of her environs. At that moment, she felt abandoned and unloved. Support and understanding was what she needed from Jan, but neither were forthcoming, only it seemed annoyance at her curiosity and indifference to her plight. Did he respect her less now she was pregnant, or was she being overly sensitive? Men were fortunate, weren't they? He could disappear out of her life forever and continue his as a 'free' spirit without responsibility, while for her she knew the struggle had just begun. If only she had not weakened, she wouldn't be in this mess now. Damn Jan and his persuasive ways. Still no use placing blame, from now on, she must go through life taking responsibility for any decisions she made, for if nothing else, this experience had taught her that she couldn't depend on others. Funny how she suddenly felt older and wiser. Her carefree days in London seemed an age removed.

They turned into a nondescript building and Jan broke the long silence, bringing Joey abruptly back to their immediate predicament.

'Here we are. Marie lives on the third floor. When we get there, I'll do most of the talking.'

'I'm so scared.'

'Of what?'

'Just everything. Marie and whatever she's going to do.'

'She's not going to do anything, so pull yourself together, Joey.'

They climbed the steep stone steps, again in silence as they went. There didn't seem to be anyone else about in the building, and for that, Joey was grateful, for she didn't want to be seen going to visit a prostitute. She silently admonished herself for these thoughts, knowing that she really wasn't any better, and for that matter, maybe not as good.

At last they had reached their destination and were waiting for a reply to the bell's discreet ring. The door, a heavy oak, groaned promptly open and there stood a pretty young lady with tumbling shoulder-length auburn curls and deep-set almond eyes. She held her hand in outstretched gesture, welcoming them into her home, at the same time planting a kiss on Jan's cheek and talking excitedly.

'Bonjour mon cher comment ca va?' then, without waiting for a reply, 'C'est Joey n'est-ce pas? Would you like some tea? Forgive me, I only speak a leetle English.'

'You're doing very well', complimented Joey, 'and it should be me apologising for not speaking French. Yes, I'd love some tea.'

Marie had quickly put Joey at her ease, and as they sat now on a comfortable rather overstuffed sofa, sipping tea with Jan and Marie puffing on cigarettes, she felt herself growing to like her hostess. She, who had always thought of these women in such a contemptuous manner, now felt ashamed that she had so readily condemned without reason. Here Joey was learning that this woman had feelings and expectations like herself. How could she have been so ignorant? She seemed to be thinking more and more like this lately as one childhood myth after another was dispelled.

Jan and Marie were talking seriously now in French, and although Joey could not understand everything, she knew that Jan was getting the information they came for. Funny, thought Joey, that Marie was so much wiser, yet she couldn't be too much older. Life itself is the best teacher of all. Jan was absolutely right; she was naïve and misinformed.

Marie quietly slipped out of the room and Jan moved closer to Joey and whispered, 'as soon as she comes back, I think we should leave.'

'Oh, she can help me then? I mean everything's going to be okay, isn't it?'

'I'll explain when we're outside.'

'Tell me now.'

'Shh, here she comes.'

Marie came back carrying a small girl about three years old.

'This is my Nicole,' she offered in response to the perplexed look on Joey's face.

'Elle est tres belle. Forgive me, Marie, Jan never told me you had a daughter.'

'Come to think about it, I didn't,' confessed Jan.

'Is there something wrong?' asked Marie.

'No, no, of course not,' stammered Joey.

At that moment, Jan took Joey by the hand and helped her from the sofa.

'We really must be leaving', he muttered, 'and thanks, Marie, for your help.' He kissed her on both cheeks in farewell and Joey noticed her slip something to him. She too then took her leave of Marie, uttering her thanks with sincerity, feeling at that moment a desire to dally awhile and learn more about this girl. Jan, however, tugged impatiently at her hand, the door closed behind them, and they were once more alone in the deserted hallway.

'Can you imagine that I was afraid to meet Marie?' said Joey half guiltily.

'Now you know how silly that was.'

'I suppose I expected a two-headed monster.' Joey laughed. 'And instead I found a warm human being. By the way, Jan, you never did tell me where you met her.'

'In one of the cafes where I played guitar.'

'Sounds familiar. Did you go to bed with her too?'

'Of course not, I wasn't sexually attracted to her. She liked our music and we liked her company.'

'When was this?'

'Oh, I guess a few years ago. Yes, sure, she was pregnant, I remember, and the boyfriend had just left her. She loved him and was devastated when it happened, so she would come into the cafe to try and forget.'

'Was she a prostitute then?'

'No, a salesgirl, but she lost her job when they knew she was pregnant.'

'How terrible for her, but why didn't she get an abortion?'

'She really wanted the child.'

'Even though she couldn't bring it up properly?'

'Who's to judge what properly means, Joey,' said Jan irritably.

'The hell you don't know, Jan. Here am I pregnant and trying to rid myself of this because we can't provide adequately.'

They were now walking through the red light district once more, but this time Joey paid little attention to the activities being carried on in the deepening shadows around her.

'I said who's to judge. Besides Marie seems to be making a very good mother.'

'You don't mean to tell me that you think that's the ideal environment for a child to grow up in.'

'She's not there all the time. Marie's mother takes care of her a good deal.'

'In other words, Marie makes a good part-time mother, and what do you think she's going to tell Nicole about her occupation when she's older?'

'Let's face it, Joey, you sound like you're trying to justify your own decision for an abortion. That's okay, I suppose, but leave Marie out of it.'

'My decision!' cried Joey indignantly. 'I like your gall. You don't seem to understand that I've been forced into this solution due to your lack of responsibility toward me and in getting a job. Don't you think I want to have my baby? How can I if I have to be the breadwinner? I don't have my mother just around the corner to run to like Marie.'

'There you go again dragging Marie into this. Why are you comparing? As for me, Joey, you knew my feelings about marriage a long time ago, and God knows I have been looking for a job. Let's not fool ourselves, neither of us is prepared to take on this responsibility right now.'

'That's not fair, Jan, I just don't have any choice. I want to be a full-time mother and have a father around for my baby.'

'That's fine, but don't blame me alone.'

'I'm not, but I can't help feeling resentment. If you were a woman, you might understand.'

'Well, I'm not, and this conversation seems to be getting us nowhere. Do you want me to tell you what Marie said? Well, she doesn't know anyone anymore who's prepared to do an abortion. Too much risk. The last person she knew who obliged for a rather large fee is in prison.'

'In prison, for what?' asked Joey.

'Well, you do know it's illegal, don't you?'

'Yes, but how was she found out?'

'The woman died, and her sister led the police right to the culprit. So Marie says everyone's lying low, not getting involved, specially where strangers are concerned. They're afraid of getting dobbed in.'

'How terrible for the woman who died I mean, but what in the world am I supposed to do now?'

'Marie gave me some pills that might help to bring on a miscarriage.'

'Oh, so that's what I saw her slip you. What happens if they don't work?'

'Marie seems to think that you might have a better chance of getting an abortion in Switzerland.'

'How? I don't know anyone there.'

'Guess you'll have to ask around, but let's wait and see if the pills work first.'

'Okay, but I'm beginning to feel really worried. I was so sure Marie would know someone that I hadn't really considered any other possibility.'

The existing feelings between Joey and Jan were certainly strained, and Joey was uncertain and afraid of their future together, if indeed there was to be one at all. This pregnancy, rather than delight Jan, had in fact had the opposite effect. Together she knew they could work out a satisfactory arrangement so she could have this baby, after all, anything's possible if you really want it. She had agreed to the abortion, not only for financial reasons, but because she was afraid of losing Jan if she didn't, and in turn, this had made her face an ugly thought that Jan's love was very tenuous indeed. However, she always quickly dismissed these thoughts and made excuses for his behaviour, rationalizing that lack of steady work was the main motivation. Yet why would he jeopardize her life in a quack's back- room office if he really held her dear?

She knew she was inexperienced with men, especially the smooth types like Jan, who could explain their way out of anything, but she still could not accept the fact that all men were so selfish. Her own dad, who treated her mother with such kindness and tenderness, was certainly not of this ilk. She surely deserved better, for hadn't she helped and encouraged Jan all along? Wasn't she now supporting him until he found a job? Or was this the trouble? She knew, though, that while he asked to be with her, she could not at this stage turn him out. He had successfully made a doormat out of her, and she was emotionally incapable of doing anything about it.

Chapter 17

Of course the pills Marie had given Joey had no effect, save for some stomach cramps. With her back now against the wall, she knew the trip to Switzerland was inevitable. Delaying this would only spoil any chances she may have of getting anyone to help her. It was already late October, and as she had only thrown up once at school, no suspicions had been aroused there.

Leaving on the evening train for Geneva, she waved goodbye to Jan, having instructed him earlier to telephone the school, advising them that she had come down with the flu, but should be back on Monday. As it was Thursday night now, this would give her two full days to get the help she needed. Beyond that, she did not wish to think.

On her arrival in Geneva, she checked into a third-rate hotel near the railway station. The room she was shown was like a horse stall and smelled nearly as badly. It didn't seem to have been aired since the hotel had been built, which to hazard a conservative guess must have been at least a century and a half before! Joey tried in vain to open the huge windows, but no amount of coaxing would budge them. The bed too had seen better days, she was sure, for the mattress was lumpy and the springs so rusted they groaned pitifully beneath her weight. In disgust, she decided to try her luck in the dining room. Here she fared better.

The cuisine, while not cordon bleu, was very palatable indeed. The veal she had ordered was tender, and the mushroom sauce delicious. It was easy tonight to forget the reason she had come to this lovely city, the wine she was drinking helped and the music coming from the piano bar soothed her mind.

She was a tourist again about to embark upon a wonderful adventure!

'Bonsoir, Mademoiselle.'

'Monsieur.'

'Permettez?'

'Mais oui.'

The young man seated himself opposite Joey at her table and called for the waiter. Joey had long since become accustomed to the practice of sharing tables with total strangers and paid little heed to this one. He ordered his dinner and she a demitasse.

'You are English?' he suddenly queried in her tongue.

'Well, Australian, how did you know?'

'Your accent for one thing, but your manners are Anglo-Saxon.'

'Really?'

'And the way you use a knife and fork, and cut your bread.'

'You are observant. I'm fond of playing those guessing games myself, but I usually look at physical features and dress.'

'I'll bet my way is more accurate than yours. Try it some time and you'll see.'

'I could start with you.' Joey laughed.

'Feel free,' he said, smiling good-humouredly.

'Ah, let me see, you broke the bread and left it sitting on the tablecloth, watered down the wine, and now to eat, you're using just a fork in your right hand. I've seen many Europeans dining that way, but you've got black hair and brown eyes, I'm unsure of your accent, so my guess is you're Italian, right?'

'Wrong, but your reasoning was good. You'll be an expert in no time, I can see. I'm French, from Paris, but I live and work here now, I'm a writer. Not too successful, I'm sorry to say, but hopeful that my luck will improve. Here's my business card to prove it. You never know when you might need a ghost writer,' he chuckled.

'Thanks and how interesting, that explains why you're so observant.'

'Oui, I think so. How about you? You're a long way from home.'

'Yes and no. You see I live and work in Cannes. A teacher of English in a French school.'

'Lucky kids, you certainly don't look like the schoolteacher type. Just as well our little guessing game didn't take in occupations, for I fear we'd both be wrong. Anyway that doesn't explain you being here in this rundown hotel, does it?'

'Just taking a long weekend for some sightseeing,' lied Joey.

'I'd be more than delighted to escort you, my time's my own.'

'Thanks, but no,' came Joey's flustered reply.

'I can assure you I'm very good company and a gentleman, in case that's what is bothering you.'

'Not at all. I just prefer to be alone when I'm a tourist. That way I don't feel guilty about dragging anyone to sights that may bore them.'

'Very well. I certainly don't want to insist. My name by the way is Jean- Claude Monteux, what's yours?'

'Joey McPhally.'

'Je suis enchante, mademoiselle, and now would you care to join me for an after-dinner drink in the bar?'

She knew she should refuse. She already felt guilty about the lie she would have to tell Jan when she returned to Cannes, and his inquisition would begin concerning each and every person she had met in Geneva. She knew how he would twist this chance meeting with Jean-Claude into an orgy.

The untruth was better than the hassle and so he would not know. What a pity he was forcing her to be like this. She, who was such an open person, now became devious, and she disliked what she was becoming. As for Jean- Claude, would he still want her company if she were to tell him the real reason for her trip to Geneva? Maybe that was going too far; after all, he had only asked her for a drink, not to marry him. They most likely would never see each other again anyway. To hell with everything, why shouldn't they have a drink and enjoy the moment?

'I'd be delighted to,' replied Joey.

Chapter 18

The next morning, Joey rose early. Her plan of action, for she knew no other way of tackling this urgent problem, was to visit as many doctors as she could with the hope of finding one who would help her.

She had heard whisperings in France, from Marie and others, that some doctors in Switzerland, where the law concerning abortions was more liberal, would render aid in hardship cases, and providing the pregnancy was not too advanced.

As is customary in many European cities, doctors tend to band together on certain streets, building next to building. Joey was more than grateful for this as she was on foot, and distance would have eaten up precious time. Now at least she could cover a number with expediency.

Her eyes scanned the brass plates as she walked, then suddenly she stopped short as she read 'Obstetrics/Gynaecology'. Her stomach turned over with nervousness, and her legs felt weak. After a moment's hesitation, she plucked up the courage to go in.

She was ushered into the waiting room by a kindly middle-aged nurse and took up her post along with some four or five others. No appointment was necessary; one was seen on a first come, first serve basis. Joey figured she had quite a long wait ahead, so she reached for a magazine to help pass the time, but found she couldn't concentrate. She was trying to figure out what she would say to the doctor. After all, she just couldn't blurt out that she wanted an abortion. He might throw her out, or worse still, turn her over to the police. She broke into a cold sweat and her mouth became very dry. Maybe it was better to leave while she still had time. She felt terrible, her heart beat rapidly, her vision was becoming blurry, and she felt nauseous.

'I need air,' she heard herself saying out loudly as she ran for the door, but didn't quite make it, as her legs turned to jelly and folded beneath her.

She came to in a small room, with the kindly nurse leaning over the table on which she was outstretched, holding smelling salts under her nose.

'That's a good girl, just a fainting spell. The doctor will be in soon,' she said soothingly in flawless English.

'Thank you, I'm okay now. Don't trouble the doctor, Nurse, I'll come back tomorrow.'

'You'll do no such thing! You're pregnant, aren't you? Didn't you come to seek prenatal care?'

'Y-yes,' faltered Joey, knowing she couldn't tell the real truth.

'Then slip on this gown so you won't keep the doctor waiting,' she commanded.

'Maybe the doctor doesn't need to examine me. You see I'd like to talk to him first,' said Joey on the verge of tears.

'You're talking nonsense, child, the doctor has to examine you, now let me help you undress.'

Joey obeyed, then the nurse left the room, leaving her sitting on the examination table nervously awaiting the doctor. She wished she hadn't let the nurse bully her into staying. Of course she had no idea why Joey was there, or that her fainting spell was brought on in part at least by her extreme anxiety.

'Oh God, how ashamed and disappointed my family would be of me now,' Joey thought. 'I really am a disgrace.'

Tears of remorse stung her eyes as she thought back fondly to her family in Australia. What absolute trust they had always had in her to make the right decisions. She knew that what she was doing would not meet with their approval, but then her whole way of life with Jan wouldn't either. She still wasn't completely free from the nest she suddenly realized, or she wouldn't be worrying about what her family thought or feel so guilt-ridden.

When the doctor came in, her body jerked and a small cry reached her lips.

'Why so edgy, my dear? I really didn't mean to startle you. Now then let me examine you first. Lie down and put your feet up in the stirrups. Good girl... now first relax, that's fine.'

The doctor's fingers probed and pushed, evoking an occasional whimper from Joey.

'Hmm... you've got a fine big baby there, and everything seems to be progressing nicely.'

Joey heard what he said, but instead of being pleased that she was carrying a healthy baby, his words made her wince. This only made it harder for her to tell the doctor what she had really come for.

'You can get up and dress now,' he said.

Nervously, Joey donned her clothes while the doctor washed his hands.

Then re-appearing from behind the screen, she quickly blurted out the truth, afraid lest her courage would leave her.

'I can't have this baby.'

The doctor, surprised by this sudden outburst, replied, 'You can't? I don't see how you can avoid having it, young lady, that's the usual outcome of a normal pregnancy, you know.'

'I know, but what I'm trying to say is, I'd hoped that I could have this pregnancy terminated.'

'How?'

'By an abortion. I heard that in certain hardship cases, a woman could get help,' said Joey.

'You do realize what you're asking? A criminal act! You have been grossly misinformed about the abortion laws of this country. No doctor worth a cent would do what you're asking of me. Anyway, what makes you think you would qualify as a hardship case, if such a law existed?'

'I'm not married, and I have no money.'

'That certainly wouldn't be grounds enough. There are lots of women in your circumstances who have their babies, it's not the end of the world.'

'For a woman in my position, it feels like it. Nobody seems to understand that, let alone care. I'm desperate, and I won't stop looking for help.'

'You are aware of the dangers that you'd be subjecting yourself to?'

'Yes, but I can't think of the consequences now.'

'What a pity you young people don't give more thought to the outcome of your actions. Did you use any contraceptives?'

'No, only the rhythm method.'

'Didn't anyone advise you that this was far from foolproof?'

'Unfortunately sex was not discussed in my house, what I learned I learned from friends.'

'Hmm, so it seems. Well, there's little else to say, except I do hope you'll reconsider and elect to keep your baby.'

Joey was no longer listening; her only thought was to get out of there as fast as possible, away from the deep humiliation she felt. Her eyes were swimming with tears as she grabbed her coat, nodded in the direction of the seated doctor, and walked out the door to the safety of the street.

From one doctor's office to the next, she presented her case. Each time she swallowed her pride and laid herself at their mercy, leaving as quickly as possible after rejection to avoid further de-moralising. In some cases, she was made to feel like a whore, in others, an irresponsible child, but in no case was any reference ever made to the other collaborator—the man! She and she alone was made to feel the entire responsibility was hers apparently because she had the physical responsibility of carrying the child, or at least that's what Joey deduced from the attitudes of these 'learned men'.

People are always great about giving advice, especially those who know the least about the way you feel, and those who for varied reasons fail to identify with your problem.

Doctors, it seemed then, were not very good counsellors, as they fit neatly into the above categories, or so Joey thought. She had read in the papers about priests' views on abortions too, and it had always angered her to read their self-righteous remarks about a subject on which they could have no knowledge whatsoever.

Whether her actions were in accordance or not with the beliefs of these different groups, she felt she alone had the right to make the ultimate decisions regarding her own body. The tears shed now were of anger, frustration, and fear. Anger because her fate rested in another's hands, and that she must feel the bite of humiliation when she should not have to. Frustration because she needed help and it was not forthcoming, and fear for what lay ahead.

Joey was weary and downhearted, her day had ended in absolute failure. She was clearly going about the entire matter the wrong way. How gullible she was to believe the medical profession would help her! She knew that out there somewhere, there had to be that 'nice' little old lady who was more than willing to help girls in distress, but how was she to find her? One had to have contacts, and her only hope, Marie, had proved useless. She was at that moment passing another gynaecologist, and although she had decided to call it quits for the day, she felt obliged to make one last effort. Bracing herself, she turned the handle of the door and briskly stepped inside.

Of course the entire interview with the doctor went along in exactly the same manner as all the previous ones had, including the examination. Joey was at a loss to understand this. Why did they bother with the ritual when they had no intention of helping? Could it be to justify their fees? The finale, however, was what made it unique, and one that Joey would no doubt remember for a lifetime. As she was about to leave, the nurse at the front desk caught her by the sleeve and, in a whisper, asked Joey to meet her in half an hour when she would be off duty at a small cafe just down the street. Joey was astonished, but agreed nonetheless. She had nothing to lose and was curious to find out what this girl was going to tell her.

At the appointed hour, they met, seated themselves to the rear of the cafe away from the rest of the patrons, and ordered Perrier.

'I know why you came to see the doctor,' said the nurse in a hushed voice.

'Oh.'

'I overheard you talking to him and I think I can help.'

'Oh great, you know someone then?'

'No, no, I don't mean help of that kind,' came the nurse's reply.

'I'm afraid I don't understand. There is no other,' said Joey in a perplexed tone.

'Yes, there is. If you have your baby, my husband and I'd adopt it.'

'You, adopt it? That's preposterous. Why, I'd never even contemplate such a thing. Anyway, why would you want to do that? You don't even know me.'

'Well, you see I can't have a baby, and we've been trying for about a year to adopt one, but the wait is endless, and the prospects slim. Sometimes I think I'll go mad with longing. I've become a nervous wreck and my marriage is becoming strained. So you see your baby would be dearly loved, and very much wanted.'

Joey caught the quiver in the nurse's voice and detected the glistening of tears in her eyes. Here was another woman who was also desperate. Oh God, didn't life play cruel tricks! Joey forgot herself for that moment and felt deep compassion for this woman who would never experience the pains of childbirth and in whose eyes was yearning. She wished sincerely that she could help her, but knew in her heart that she would have to turn her down.

'I understand how you feel, and I appreciate your offer. For someone else, it might have been the right solution, but it isn't for me,' said Joey. 'I know if I bore this child, I would never be able to part with it.'

'You prefer to kill it then? Is that what you're saying?' came the nurse's challenging remarks.

'Of course not,' retorted Joey.

'Well, what is it then? I beg of you to reconsider,' pleaded the distraught nurse.

'My mind is made up,' said Joey brusquely. 'I cannot help you and now I must be leaving.'

As Joey prepared to go, the nurse whispered, 'You will be punished one day for this sin.'

Night was beginning to descend on Geneva, and a brisk wind set tavern signs in groaning motion, and debris was whipped along city streets to cling at last to wall and fence. Joey quickened her pace, buttoned up her coat, and this time headed determinedly for her hotel. She covered ground without really being aware, for her mind was occupied. The audacity of this nurse to suggest murder. She for one had certainly never looked upon it as such, and this girl was the first who had blatantly said so. It angered Joey, for she felt she already had enough to contend with without heaping more guilt on her. She had received no sympathy and felt wretched and dejected. If only she could talk to someone who would understand. She longed for the closeness and friendship she'd had with Amy. There was someone in whom she could confide and receive solace in return... or could she? No, her lifestyle would be so alien to Amy that for her to understand would require a miracle. This, of course, was the reason that Joey never divulged her private life in any of her correspondence to people who had once shared her secrets and intimacies. Yet in analysis that seemed only to be a half-truth, with the remaining shrouded in shame. There was little doubt she had changed. It became increasingly clear to Joey this change was for the worse. She could not bear to be unmasked by those she loved, and so her life had become wrapped in secrecy. That was the reason for her aloneness now.

Joey reached the hotel in time for dinner, but decided to go straight to her room instead. She certainly didn't feel hungry; neither did she want to run into Jean-Claude. After such a day, she could not face him without some tell-tale signs of her ordeal, and this she wanted to avoid.

In fact she wanted to be rid of this city as quickly as possible and decided to return to Cannes a day earlier. There was no sense in wasting further time or money here, for she was sure help, if it were forthcoming, would be from a source yet untapped and so far unknown to her. Back in Cannes, she again would try to discover other possibilities, which would inevitably lead her to her goal. She would not fail!

Chapter 19

Easter holidays were almost upon Joey and not before time! She was under great strain from the demands of her job and the feelings of panic that plagued her concerning her ever-swelling abdomen, as she was nearly five months pregnant. It was also growing increasingly difficult to function effectively at school, as her mind was constantly on personal problems.

Jan had eventually obtained work as an export manager with a flower company. He didn't like his work particularly, but seemed to enjoy the extra money he could jingle in his pocket. Joey realized this and felt renewed pangs of insecurity. She had grown used to Jan's dependence on her and felt threatened now by his financial freedom. If for any reason he felt inclined to leave her, now would be the time. There was always that uncertainty, day in and day out. Of course she could be the one to do the leaving, but as her feelings for Jan were genuine, there wasn't much likelihood of it happening, and she knew Jan was conscious of this. Even though he had always made a point of expressing his love for her, Joey realised what a restless person Jan was and that his words of the present may not match his feelings in the future. In fact, it was rare to find his words and actions in harmony. Joey felt justified in her concern.

With him, there could be only today. This revelation saddened her, as she felt a commitment of longer than just a day at a time was necessary to sustain any relationship.

Love, trust, respect, and friendship needed long- term nourishment, without which they would surely die. There had to be a tomorrow to look forward to and to justify the hardships or joys of today. Happily her vocation still promised her a tomorrow, and for now, that must do.

Since her return from Geneva, Joey had feverishly sought the elusive abortionist. She had gone back to see Marie alone, hoping that a womanly confrontation might extract more information, but she was wrong. Marie was very sympathetic, by far the most understanding of anyone Joey had talked to so far, but she couldn't give her any concrete help. She did, however, pass on a tip that proved to be very valuable.

'Talk to men, and ask them,' she advised.

'But I don't know any... at least none that I could discuss this with.'

'Then go out and find some, strangers, anyone, so long as they're men.' 'Oh, I could never do that,' whimpered Joey.

'You'll have to, and you'd better hurry,' came Marie's advice.

Joey spent time in some of the local cafes, with the intent of cornering any male that looked as though he might be in possession of the information she desired. When the time appeared right for her to start up a conversation with the unsuspecting man, she suddenly felt shy and timid, and the moment was lost. In a way, she thought it was just as well, as she didn't know how she could ask such a question of a total stranger. She wondered where all the men who had approached her in the past were hiding. They certainly would help her plight right now, at least by making the first move, which Joey still could not bring herself to do, despite the gravity of the situation. After all, they were bound to misinterpret her overtures, and if there was anything she wished to avoid, it was giving men the wrong idea. She was sure Marie would know how to handle this, but she herself was totally inept.

He suddenly crossed her mind, Jean-Claude Monteux! The man she had met in Geneva. Thank goodness he had handed her his business card the first night they met, for he had given her the impression of knowing his way around—observant, knowledgeable, mature. Yes, she would write to him and find out if he could help her. This way she wouldn't have to confront him either, or at least not initially. What a pity though, she had liked him and didn't want him to be involved in this side of her life, or rather, she didn't want him to think of her as a tramp. She had no choice though, he would have to know.

Of course Joey knew she must keep Jean-Claude a secret from Jan. She knew there would only be ugly accusations followed by fights. She had not breathed a word about meeting him in Geneva and she would give the school address for any correspondence in order to avert trouble.

Chapter 20

It was on a beautiful spring morning a week later that Joey's secrecy dealt her a cruel blow. She and Jan were preparing to go out when Madame Gilbert came to the door with a letter for Joey. The instant her eyes swept the envelope, she knew it was a reply from Jean-Claude. Too late to hide it, Jan had already seen and was moving towards her to find out who it was from.

'Who's Jean-Claude Monteux?' he queried as he read the name off the envelope.

'Just someone I know.'

'Just someone you know? Is that any answer?'

'I'd rather not talk about it right now.'

'Why not? What are you hiding, Joey?'

'Nothing! I'd just like my mail to remain mine, that's all,' she said with irritation.

'Come on, let me see it,' he said, lunging towards her.

Joey instinctively hid the letter behind her back and out of the reach of Jan's hands. He was not to be deterred though, and the more Joey resisted, the more adamant he became about taking the letter from her. Finally he had her cornered with one arm twisted behind her back, wriggling and squealing in pain.

'Let me go, damn you, you're hurting!'

'Not till you give me the letter,' said Jan sternly. 'No,' she screamed, enraged now by Jan's insistence.

She began kicking and scratching at Jan like a wild thing trapped by her own guilt and the knowledge that there was no easy way out. Slowly she sank exhausted to the floor and resisted no further, so Jan took the crumpled letter from her sweaty palm and triumphantly began reading it.

'So you did lie to me then. You did meet a man in Geneva after all.' 'You almost sound pleased,' came Joey's weak response.

'Of course I'm not pleased to find out I can't trust you. You disappoint me. What did you have to do to get this guy to help you, seduce him, eh?'

'If that's what you want to believe, but that's not what happened.' 'Well, why did you keep it such a big secret then?'

'Because I knew you wouldn't believe me anyway. You seem to take a perverted delight in twisting my words. I don't know why you think that every meeting with every male always ends in bed!'

'Why else do you think they're interested in you?'

'Thanks, Jan, coming from you, that's really great! I thought I had a few other worthwhile qualities that might make me of interest. Maybe the truth is that's all you see in me, don't want to marry, or care what happens to our baby? The more I think, the more I'm convinced you don't love me at all.'

'Don't let's start that again.'

'Why not, it's the truth, isn't it? Why do you think I have to write to other people for help because you don't give a damn? Do you know what I went through in Geneva to try to get us both out of this mess and all you can do is accuse me of some nonsense? I'm really getting fed up with being falsely blamed, and it's time you knew. I'm not always questioning what you do. You're probably the one who's sleeping around if only the truth were known and then passing your guilt off on me.'

'Shut up, Joey,' he yelled, slapping her across the face.

'How dare you hit me,' cried Joey hysterically. 'Get out of here, I never want to see you more.'

'Okay, if that's the way you feel, I will, but you'll be sorry, you'll never find anyone like me again.' And he stormed towards the door.

'Just give me my letter and the door key, and leave me in peace.' Jan tossed them on the bed and was out the door and gone.

Joey heard his footsteps retreating along the garden path, and then the clang of the large iron gate closing brought a sense of finality to their romance. Joey instantly regretted her actions, which were aroused in passion, but was too proud to chase after him and beg forgiveness. After all, he had raised his hand to her and she could not let him get away with it.

Joey wept silently at first till the full impact of facing life without him registered on her numbed brain, which set her to sobbing uncontrollably.

She buried her face deeper in her hands and rocked back and forth in helpless motion. She wanted to cry out and let the world know that she couldn't go on alone. The magnitude of her problems suddenly seemed so much greater. Oh, the misery of it all, Joey thought as she threw herself onto her bed and cried until every tear was spent.

The emotional stress she had gone through with Jan had just been too debilitating. She didn't want to suffer in this way again.

The letter from Jean-Claude, which she now took in trembling hands, contained good news. He could help her and, as he would be visiting friends in Cannes the following weekend, would be glad to take her back to Geneva with him on the Sunday night, if she could make it. The timing for Joey couldn't have been better, as it coincided with Easter. He went on to let her know too that he would be happy to drive her back again after her business was completed.

'God bless him,' Joey whispered.

This news perked her spirits a little, and she decided to answer the letter immediately. As she got paper and pen, she thought about the chain of events that had led her up to this moment. Her introduction to Marie, by Jan whose advice to seek a man's aid had resulted in Jean-Claude's letter. In turn, the school had obviously forwarded it on to Joey with kind intent, to eventually cause the break between Jan and herself. Weird how things worked out. The very help she and Jan so desperately needed had separated them when it arrived, solely because the assistance was being given in part by a man. Her scheme had backfired and now she was alone. It seemed to her that she was damned no matter what she did. When this nasty business was over, she assured herself, she would begin to put her life back together again. She would be as good as new, and no one would be any the wiser she conjectured, as she began her reply to Jean-Claude.

Dear Diary,

The Parting Gift
A heart rent with sadness,
An eye no longer so bright,
A tongue rendered speechless,
Am I as I say goodbye.
No more to see your face,
Or to touch your body close,
Instead an empty place,
Left inside of my soul.
I leave you now, my love,
With all I have to impart,
Only my gleaming teardrops,
Wrapped up in my broken heart.

J. McP.

Chapter 21

Joey was once more installed in the same hotel as on her previous trip to Geneva. The room was not the same though, as she had particularly requested another, and had been given one more to her liking, less stall-like and fresher in fragrance. She was preparing now for bed after a long and tiring trip by car from Cannes.

She had met Jean-Claude as pre-arranged and had passed the journey in idle conversation, travelling via the tortuous roadway through Grenoble onward to Geneva. Joey had become car sick en route and had asked on several occasions to be let out. Jean-Claude had obliged without complaint, in fact Joey found him a most compliant and amiable person. The subject of her trip was not broached, no questions were asked, not even a reproachful glance given, no hint at all from him that he was aware of the plight of his passenger. So convincing had his silence on the subject been that Joey felt prompted to suddenly ask, in case there had been a gross misunderstanding between them.

'You haven't really told me yet where we're actually going or what arrangements have been made.'

His reply came cool and soothing. 'I can assure you, Joey, that I have taken the necessary steps on your behalf and that tomorrow we'll arrive at the rendezvous.'

'Can't you tell me where that is?'

'No, you'll know soon enough. Trust me, Joey, it's best for all concerned. Remember, abortions are illegal.'

'Yes, of course.' Joey nodded in understanding.

They were driving to the outskirts of Geneva, the city now captured in the rear-view mirror fell further behind them, till only the tallest church steeples were visible. Ahead of them lay sprawling villages, nestled in grassy foothills, which were flanked on all sides by proud peaks. These sights finally gave way to pastures freshly strewn with spring flowers and dotted with munching cows, sporting tinkling bells dangling from their necks. The farm buildings with their bright coats of red paint became more numerous, and the scents of fresh grass and blooms blotted out any remnants of city smells still lingering on the breeze.

Spring, a time of rebirth, seemed incongruous with Joey's mission and its blatant abuse to nature's plan. These subtleties escaped her attention, however, as she silently gazed out of the window at the storybook farms now passing at alarming speed.

Abruptly Jean-Claude swung the car off the main highway onto a small dirt road, raising clouds of dust and mild profanities from Joey. They bumped and jerked along for what seemed an eternity before Jean-Claude pointed out their destination. It was not unlike the other farmhouses they had seen, save perhaps for its isolation, well tucked in from the main highway. As they drew nearer though, Joey could detect a number of people busily working in the fields. Some were bent over attending to the soil, while others were herding animals into small fenced pens. The scene was an active one as each person went about his chores, oblivious of anyone around him. Only a cow or two looked up from feeding and nodded its head, as if in welcome, as they entered the tree-lined private road leading to the comfortable-looking farmhouse.

With introductions behind her, and pleasantries exchanged with a couple in their late fifties, Joey was led away by the grandmotherly lady to a spare bedroom. It was situated on the ground floor next to the kitchen, which had probably served as a maid's quarter at one time. With their intrusion, the floorboards groaned ominously as if they knew the purpose of this invasion and were showing their disapproval. A shiver ran through Joey.

Deftly the lady went to work and, in short time, had inserted a foreign object into Joey's vaginal passage and on into the womb. She winced with pain as the lady performed her task. This satisfactorily completed, without asking any questions about the procedure, Joey was escorted back to the kitchen. Here they joined Jean-Claude and the grandfatherly gentleman for a cup of coffee, as though nothing had happened, save for the great discomfort Joey felt.

No words had been exchanged between the two women, only a smile and a nod of understanding from the old lady. The reason, of course, was the lack of a common language between them. In spite of this, Joey was confident and at ease with her, although, due to her own ignorance, she had no idea what was supposed to happen next. She silently hoped Jean-Claude, now in conversation with the lady, would be able to explain this to her.

Joey had been kept pretty much in the dark, concerning her fate, and relied entirely upon Jean-Claude's negotiations. She obeyed his orders without question, trusting his judgments in this matter completely. When they had finished their coffee, and he made motions to take leave of the couple, she complied, although surprised by his actions, thinking she would be staying there.

Once on the highway heading back to Geneva, Jean-Claude explained everything to Joey.

'The procedure you had should bring about a miscarriage in a relatively short time.'

This left Joey open-mouthed in disbelief at the simplicity of the scheme.

'You'll remain at your hotel in Geneva until labour begins, and then we'll return to the farm hideaway,' explained Jean-Claude. 'Apparently the old lady doesn't want you in her house any longer than necessary, lest your presence gives rise to suspicion among the farmhands.'

'Thanks for explaining all of this to me and for being so attentive.' 'That's fine. I'm happy to help out.'

To speed up the process, Joey had to walk briskly about. Jean-Claude never left her side, marching her endlessly along the riverbanks. By nightfall, Joey was exhausted, and she sensed a dull ache in the pelvic region. Bloodstains had appeared and Joey felt uneasy at the sight, for she wasn't sure if all was going as it should be. Jean-Claude noted her alarm and insisted on remaining with her during the night.

They stretched out together, fully clothed on top of the large old iron bedstead, hoping at least for some rest, as sleep seemed elusive. Joey's pain had intensified, and a fever now flushed her forehead. Jean-Claude lay quietly, with body tensed in case of an emergency, opening a wary eye from time to time to make sure she was okay.

Joey twisted and turned restlessly. She felt sick and frightened at what yet lay ahead, but in spite of her misery at that moment, she was able to really see through half-closed eyes this total stranger beside her. For in truth, that was all he was and yet what a comfort he'd become. He certainly was a handsome man with a firm jawline, dark wavy hair, and an athletic body. She'd often heard tell that casual acquaintances were more apt to lend money in a time of crisis, where close ties inevitably were strained or even broken when the same demands were made of them. She certainly didn't know this would apply to these circumstances as well.

Jean-Claude stood to gain nothing by his philanthropic acts, which made him unique. Inspired by tenderness, she took his hands in hers and brushed them with her lips, snuggling closer to him in gratitude, for the concern and caring his warm body transmitted to hers. In response, he wrapped a protective arm about her, cradling her head on his shoulder. She felt calm and secure, and better able to cope with her pain, and thus together they passed the night.

Midday saw them once more at the farm. Joey this time was promptly hustled away to the spare bedroom by the woman, who seemed impatient to have this deed behind her. Joey perceived a trembling of her fingers as she carried out the examination. A knot of fear suddenly tugged at Joey's breast, afraid that something might go wrong. However, she had come this far and knew there was no turning back!

With examination complete, Joey spent the rest of the afternoon walking along the country roads with Jean-Claude.

Chapter 22

The stillness of the house was pierced by shrill cries of agony from Joey. Her body writhed in pain, and beads of sweat stood out like marbles on her brow. Her clenched hands showed rows of white knuckles, and her fingernails dug deeply into her palms. Blood spurted down her thighs, soaking her nightdress and bed linen. Her hair hung wet and matted around her face, and her eyes smarted with tears. She was just able to catch her breath before the next onslaught of pain overwhelmed her. The spasms up until now had been bearable, and Joey had managed very well. In fact, she had paced the bedroom floor until these latest seizures had forced her onto the bed, where she could no longer control her writhing or screaming. She continued on in this way for what seemed to be an eternity, her cries getting louder and louder, until with a mighty contraction and scream to match, Joey felt the baby's head expelled. She managed to roll off the bed and squat, legs apart over a large basin, which had been set in the room for the sole purpose of receiving the foetus. A few minutes later and the baby was totally ejected into the bowl.

Joey's last scream had brought the old lady quickly to her side, too late to

help or render any comfort! Together they gazed on this stillborn baby girl. Joey quickly turned her head away, while the old lady cried, 'Mon dieu!'

A few minutes later, the scene took on that of a criminal covering all of his tracks as carefully as possible, as the old lady went about wrapping the evidence for disposal. She left the room with her bundle, but returned shortly thereafter empty-handed.

A broken-hearted Joey, shaken and exhausted from her ordeal, fell back to bed. She must get as much rest as possible now, for tomorrow she would leave with Jean-Claude for Cannes.

She knew for the first time in her life what it was like to do something really wicked and that she would have to live with the guilt. The nurse in Switzerland had been right that she would be punished. She not only felt great bitterness towards Jan, but swore to a life of chastity in the future. Never again would she allow a man to use her in the way he had!

Spring

Diary

Dear God,
Forgive me for I have sinned.

J. McP.

The next day, as Joey bade farewell to Jean-Claude at her lodgings in Cannes, she suddenly asked, 'Why did you help me?'

Speaking softly, he replied, 'A cousin of mine in similar circumstances to yours ended her life tragically. I couldn't ignore your plight.'

Spontaneously, Joey put her arms around him and planted a gentle kiss on his cheek in gratitude for his help and many kindnesses. Each promised the other they would write. Joey gave him her parents' address in Cardellum, in case he ever made a trip Down Under, but knew this was unlikely. The need that had brought them together was no more. He was the kind of person who came into one's life for a fleeting moment, to be snatched back to obscurity the next after lending a helping hand. One was always the richer for having known someone like this. She felt sad, too, at losing him before having really known him, but was glad to keep his happy memory at least.

Now alone in her room, Joey let loose a flood of tears. She felt an enormous amount of self-pity and disgust, but most of all, the emptiness of her life was what disturbed her. Would she ever be able to have the 'normal' personal life she so wanted?

Chapter 23

Joey was in the midst of packing—the first step to divorce herself completely from her life and memories in Cannes. She had to leave her quarters due to her decision not to return to Madame Girot for another school year. She was now almost penniless, and the sensible thing to do was to accept the offer of a tent from the parents of another teacher who were camped in a trailer park in Cap D'Antibes. This way she could pass the summer in beautiful surroundings and then return to London in September in time to get school work there.

She had not seen Jan again since he had walked out, and as time had passed, she realized that her decision to leave for England was the right one. Joey still loved him very much, but knew he was not right for her. She was pleased she was able to make this decision to leave, made of course less difficult by his absence, but nonetheless, she had proved to herself that she was still strong and able to act independently. Some people in the same circumstances might have waited around, hoping he would show up again, and the fact that she didn't do this made her proud.

It was with more hope and optimism for the future then that Joey moved into her tent at Cap D'Antibes. Her furnishings were sparse, but sufficient, and consisted of a couple of suitcases which would double up as tables, an army cot, and a reed mat to cover the earth floor. The tent was surprisingly comfortable, except at midday, when the sun beat down unmercifully and the air inside would become stifling. Joey headed for a swim at that time and so escaped the heat.

Due to the generosity of her colleague's parents, she was summoned for a cup of tea every morning, which turned out to be sweeter than nectar, and a ritual on which Joey began to rely as her only source of early morning refreshment. The amusing thing about this ritual, however, was the manner in which she was received with great cordiality, like it was a once-a-year party, and then the way she in turn played surprised and taken aback by the sudden invitation! Of course this was done to let Joey know subtly that she should not take it for granted, which of course it was by all concerned.

Joey's last small pay cheque from Madame Girot would cover only the barest essentials. So she subsisted on a whole ripe tomato, lettuce, cheese, and a raw onion baguette sandwich, followed by a piece of fruit and some milk. This became pretty well her daily menu for lunch and dinner, except for an occasional splurge at a cheap fish cafe, for the three months she was to be at the camp ground. Yes, there were other choices of food at the camp's store, but as Joey's work permit had come to an end at the termination of her contract, she needed to be frugal. Needless to say, she lost weight, and her face became gaunt, but otherwise she remained fairly fit.

In spite of the apparent physical hardship of her existence, Joey enjoyed the solitude and communing with nature, which had a soothing and healing effect on her. She took daily walks along the shores of the inviting

Mediterranean and snorkelled in its warm aqua waters delighting, as she dived beneath the waves, the spectacle of colourful fish, which played hide- and-seek among the sun-filtered seaweed and then darted inquisitively around her.

She thought often and hard about Jan and at times would have run to him if she had known where he was. These moments passed, however, and Joey was able to think about her future again as a single woman.

The prospects of returning to London now held and fascinated her thoughts. To visit old friends once more and feel the beat of the city streets beneath her feet excited and helped her forget recent trials and unhappiness. Joey's relatively calm state brought her once more in closer touch with her family back in Australia. She began to write more frequently, though she never divulged to them any problems. Her letters were always cheerful, continuing the belief that what they didn't know couldn't hurt or worry them. She, of course, had become most adept at this, since she had left home.

While she had previously felt sapped of her energies, due to the emotional demands of her job and the complete and undivided attention Jan had commanded, she now, in contrast, felt revitalized. Her body was recovered from the recent abortion and her mind free to pursue her dreams.

She had taken to lying on her cot in the cool summer evenings and wondered where life was leading her. It seemed that events and circumstances kept popping up over which she had very little control, forcing her to move with this unseen hand. It was a lovely feeling in one way to be spirited off, but also frightening and maybe dangerous. She stopped herself short in the middle of one such reverie to listen more intently to a noise she had heard outside the tent. She almost stopped breathing in an attempt to muffle her now-quickened breaths. She heard it again—footsteps just by the tent door. Then an all-too-familiar voice, that of Jan whispering her name, 'Joey.'

'Oh, Jan, you scared the life out of me!'

'Can I come in?'

'I can't see how I can stop you, considering there's only a zipper separating us,' Joey answered shakily at the prospects of seeing him again.

Then he was in, standing tall and blond and as handsome as she remembered. He took her hands in his and kissed her forehead. At that moment, all the bitterness she had felt for him disappeared, and the feelings of tenderness she had harboured filled her being.

'I've never had you out of my mind for a moment, you know,' he confessed.

'I can hardly believe that. You didn't even bother to find out about the abortion,' she replied without bitterness.

'If you only knew the hell I've been through. Of course I worried.'

'Why didn't you come and see me then? God knows, Jan, I felt so alone.'

Tears of remembrance swept her cheeks, and Jan put his arm round her shoulders comfortingly.

'I really don't know why, Joey, but I just couldn't. I kept seeing your face when you told me to get out, and I just figured you wouldn't want to see me.'

'Maybe it was just as well, I did feel awfully bitter towards you, Jan.'

'You don't hate me anymore then?'

'I guess not. I probably hate myself more.'

'What do you mean?'

'For what I've done. The abortion. Jan, you'll never know what that did to me, I don't think I can adequately describe my feelings of horror and guilt.'

'Well, you certainly can't go through life blaming yourself. I'm sure you'll forget the whole thing given time.'

'That's easy to say, but I'm not at all sure. You know, Jan, there was a young nurse in Geneva who offered to adopt the baby.'

'And?'

'And naturally I refused, but it's what she said that bothered me.' 'What was that?'

'She insinuated I was a murderess and said I'd be punished. You know, Jan, I'd never even thought about abortion like that before, but when I look back on it, I'm beginning to think she was right. That's the frightening thing, if she was right about that, maybe about being punished will also come true.'

'That's nonsense and you know it. Of course, you only did what you thought was right at the time, and nobody can be blamed for that. Can we now forget it and talk about something else?'

Typical of Jan not to want to discuss anything unsavoury that might implicate him in any way.

'I heard from Stig and Ingrid. Guess what, they married!' said Jan, changing the subject.

'Great, I had a feeling they might. Where does that leave you, Jan?'

'No more guitar playing, I guess. Sad thought, but I've still got my job, so I'll be okay. But what's this I hear about you leaving? I can't believe you're really going to abandon me, Joey, after all we've meant to each other.'

'After our separation, I realized you're not the man for me, so I've decided to go back to England and work there for a while until I'm sure of what I should do next.'

'Not the man for you, but that's ridiculous: We love each other, don't we?'

'I'm not sure about your love anymore, Jan, but whatever we've got, it's destructive. We only hurt each other, and what's the good of a love like that?' Joey surprised herself at the tone of her own words, sounding so sure, while inside she hurt badly. She was again confused as always, when he was with her, and felt a touch of resentment that he had come back to upset her tranquillity and plans. However, she was strong and determined that this time he would not weaken her. She felt safe in the knowledge anyway that no matter how persuasive he was, without her job, she would have to leave.

'So you really do intend to leave me then?' Jan continued.

'Yes, as a matter of fact, in a few weeks.'

'Then we don't have too much time. So can't we be friends till then?' he asked in an irresistible tone.

'I guess there's no harm in that, so long as that's all.'

'Of course that's all. What do you take me for?' he added with a mischievous gleam in his eye. 'I propose we go to have a nice dinner, with wine and candlelight, and catch up on all our doings.'

'Sounds great,' replied Joey, who had eaten nothing but sandwiches for weeks. 'By the way, Jan, who told you where I was, and how did you get here?'

'Ah-ha, our dear friend Madame Gilbert. She's even distressed about our split-up. She thought we were the perfect couple', he teased, 'and thanks to the generosity of my company, I have the use of their car.'

'Marvellous,' laughed Joey, caught up in the spirit of the moment.

Here was Jan being his old charming self again. He was so easy to love. There would be plenty more girls' hearts broken, Joey was sure, long after she would be no more than a distant memory. The only way to forget him, or at least ease her pain, was definitely to set miles between them and so physically prevent him from turning up on her doorstep. While she remained in a position for him to do that, she would never be free from his grasp.

They saw each other again every day, in spite of rather weak protestations from Joey. He had once more entrapped her by his charm, just the way he had the first time. Her resistance weakened, until finally it broke down and she found herself in bed with him again! She was no better protected this time either and felt stupid that she could allow herself to be so cajoled. Joey was more confused than ever now as her heart and mind conflicted. She even realized how much kinder in the long run it would be if someone— anyone—would physically come and snatch her from Jan's grasp. Not so much that she needed to be protected from him, but rather from herself. She was her own worst enemy now as she lacked self-trust. It seemed she was strong in most everything else, but this relationship defied her every reason. It became clearer to Joey that what she had previously believed to be a show of strength, in taking the initiative, and quitting her job, in fact had only been achieved because he had not been there to influence her.

Jan had made her imminent departure so much more difficult again. For unlike a man, physical intimacy generally deepens the feelings in a woman for the man she loves, making parting much more painful.

'Why', Joey thought, 'does he torment me so? Is it just the sense of power he wields over me that he enjoys? How can he be so cruel?'

She knew him well enough by now to know they could continue on like this forever, if she permitted it. Horrible thought! Her salvation lay only in her physical retreat from him. Sooner or later, she would recover completely from this disastrous union, where she had been reduced to a puppet, jerked into action at Jan's bidding, a mere plaything.

She was so relieved she had given up her job, for if left until now, she would never have been able to do it!

Chapter 24

The sadness of her parting from Jan in Cannes, now behind her, Joey bravely stepped down from the train at Victoria station, ready to start life afresh. They had promised each other they would write, and Joey had cried a lot as the train departed, leaving a dry-eyed, but sad-faced Jan. Funny how she would remember that time with clarity, even as the years rolled by. She was sure her soul died that day, for even in retrospect, she could feel how part of her had seemed to drain away, leaving an emptiness that she knew could not be readily dispelled. A former colleague had written later to let her know that Jan was seen walking hand in hand with another girl, the very night she had left!

She hurried through the pressing crowds at the station as night was rapidly approaching and she had to find lodgings. Red-cap porters sought to extract the luggage from her hands, but Joey hung on to them tenaciously, fearful of the tip she would have to pay.

Approached by one of these porters, she had to smile to herself when she found her short retort to his gesture came out in rather good French. Joey had become so thoroughly immersed in this language that she'd even begun dreaming in it. Not surprising then that this should come automatically, with English still sounding weird to her almost French ears!

Hailing a taxi, she bade the driver to take her to Earl's Court. This after all was the section of London she knew well, and she therefore decided would be the best point from which to begin her pursuit of 'digs'. She requested to be set down in the busy shopping district, for past experience had shown windows filled with small notices, advertising such things as holidays, autos for sale, help wanted, vacant bedsitters, etc.

She left the cabbie muttering under his breath about those stingy Froggies. Her tip had been meagre, and yes, she had again responded in French, but this time had indeed been taken for a native.

With nose pressed against a shop windowpane, Joey copied down four bedsitter vacancies, then hurried to a telephone to make the necessary enquiries. She was successful at the fourth try, and soon found herself at her new home, which was not unlike the one she had lived in before.

Recapturing the mood of London was a happy time for Joey, but once accomplished, she felt that nagging loneliness setting in. She no longer knew anyone closely, for she soon found out that many of her old acquaintances had moved away. Things were different even after only two years!

The work in her new school was pleasant, but now after two months in London, she had formed no new ties with anyone. The hardest hours to get through were the evenings. She was alone, with no telephone or television to temporarily divert her melancholy, just books and her thoughts. She did find herself spending more time at her correspondence and had already written a number of cards to Jan, but no letter or word from him in response. In spite of her growing preoccupation with mail deliveries and resulting sadness, she found none bearing his all-too-familiar handwriting. This, of course, only served to confirm her past belief in his insincerity.

'Imagine', she said out loudly, 'if I had a child now!'

Her loneliness deepened, and she was aware of her vulnerability to anyone who might wish to take advantage of her while in this state. She did not have to wait long before such a situation presented itself. Joey was facing the prospect of another bleak Saturday evening at home alone, when there came a knock at her door. She opened it to confront an attractive young man.

'Sorry to disturb you', he muttered, 'but I wonder if you have an iron I might borrow? Mine's broken.'

'Sure', came Joey's prompt reply, then as an afterthought, she added, 'please come in.'

He did, and in no time, Joey was putting the iron into his hands, saying, 'Keep it as long as you like.'

'Thanks, but I'm moving tomorrow. Just want to iron a shirt for my trip.' 'Oh, going anywhere exciting?'

'Glasgow, if you call that exciting. It's a job transfer.' 'I haven't seen you before,' a perplexed Joey said.

'Probably because I'm not often at home. To tell the truth, I didn't even know who lived in this room, or for that matter, any of the bedsits. I'm from across the hallway,' he said, indicating with his finger.

'I wondered who rented there,' confessed Joey.

'Well, we still have this evening to get acquainted. Care to have a drink with me later?' he said seductively.

Joey knew what was implied by the invitation, but found herself accepting in spite of the risks involved and for all the other level-headed reasons that should have made her decline. She desperately needed the companionship of another human being and so replied, 'Sounds fine.'

'See you in about an hour then,' he said and was gone, taking the iron with him.

Later that night, Joey lay in bed thinking over the events that had earlier taken place between her and her neighbour. It bothered her to know that she could go to bed with a man whose name she'd not troubled to find out, about whom she knew nothing, save for his attractive face and body, and who was leaving the next day for a distant city. How indifferent she had been, how unfeeling! Jan's accusations of her whorish qualities, certainly if not true then, were true now, or so Joey believed as she wrestled with her thoughts.

She must have dozed off, for quite suddenly she was wrenched from sleep's clutches by her mother's voice distinctly calling her name. She opened her drowsy eyes and listened intently—yes, she heard it again! Then from beneath the sleepy lids, she perceived a spinning ball of light coming through her window towards the bed. Trembling and afraid, she sat up with the covers up under her chin. Her name came clearly from out of the ball of light, getting larger and larger as it approached, hovering over her as the voice whispered her name again. There was absolutely no mistaking her mother's call—just as Joey remembered it from childhood, when her mother gave her reassurance in times of unhappiness. Once more, here she was at her side in her loneliness, in unearthly form, soothing her troubled spirit by her comforting voice projected from afar. As mysteriously as the ball of light had come, it vanished through the bedroom wall, leaving Joey shaking at the reality of this phenomenon, but quieter of spirit.

At a later time in a letter, Joey mentioned this remarkable incident to her mother, who quickly confirmed that on that day and at that precise time, she had been thinking deeply about her.

Of course after this vision, Joey wondered why she just didn't pack up and go home to those she loved. Surely this would be the best route?

However, deep down inside, she knew she wasn't ready to make permanent this separation from Jan. She dearly hoped the day was not too far off, however, when release from this impossible love affair would come and give her another chance at life.

Chapter 25

The prospect of spending Christmas alone in London plagued Joey day and night. The fact that everyone else would be gathering for family reunions, and the fun they would have in decorating their trees and exchanging gifts, made her sense of loneliness more acute and unbearable. Enterprising as she was, and forever the optimist, Joey began to seek a solution. She always believed in her own ability to alter the course or outcome of any situation she found herself in, providing she was alone and in full charge.

One Sunday morning in November, warmly clad against the cold, Joey set out with the *London Times* under her arm and made for her favourite weekend haunt—Regent's Park—to scrutinise the paper at her leisure.

She enjoyed this place very much, for there was always a lot going on, and it was free entertainment at that! The English are a hardy race of people, and it had amused Joey to see them walking or sitting with blankets drawn up under their noses, inhaling deeply, and generally enjoying the great outdoors in spite of the cold. In fact, a friend of hers who lived in Surrey had, in the depth of winter, put her infant outside in her pram in order for it to get plenty of fresh air! Joey now found herself sharing in their madness! People-watching too was a favourite pastime, and here she could be amused for hours, especially on occasions when speakers would arrive carrying orange crates, which would serve as platforms for lively speeches on every topic imaginable.

Taking a colourful deck chair, Joey positioned it so as to take advantage of the weak rays of sunshine. She then opened up the paper to the personal column, which never failed to intrigue her, and had become her most thoroughly read section. It was from here that she hoped to decide what would occupy her time during the festive season. It was exciting not knowing what you were looking for, nor caring, as long as it struck your fancy. She ran her finger down the page, coming across ads for missing persons, free pregnancy tests, holidays in the south of France, remedies for drinking problems, and even a husband wanted by an attractive fiftyish widow! Joey's lips curled with a smile.

Just before the end of the column, she found a notice that seemed just right for her. One more person was needed to complete a group going on a package-deal skiing trip to Austria for one week at Christmas. Although she had never skied, the idea sounded fun and just the thing to take her blues away.

Joey was successful when, a few nights later, she met with a young married couple who were the group leaders. The chemistry seemed just right between them, and without too much of an inquisition, the marrieds decided she would complement the party most satisfactorily. Joey also learned there would be six people altogether in their group, four men and two women, and their destination was to be the small alpine village of Damüls, which would be reached by train, and finally, a bus up to the hotel. They breathed the crisp, clean air as they hurried from their bus at the rustic hotel in Damüls.

Unfortunately, sunshine had melted a good deal of the snow. Seeing the looks of disappointment on their faces, the hotel owner, who had personally stepped outside to welcome them, assured all that good skiing conditions in fact did exist, but on the higher slopes.

Joey's hotel room was small, but pleasantly furnished, with an oversized bed dominating and a massive downy quilt thrown over it, as European as the demitasse. These covers always made Joey feel like being submerged beneath another mattress! An old-fashioned wardrobe, dresser, and bedside tables with lamps completed the furnishings. The walls were covered with a floral paper, lending cosiness to the room, and finally rose-strewn carpeting padded the floors. The shuttered windows in fact were double, two sets of glass to deter the bitter cold, and upright steam pipes, now making weird sounds, tended to overheat the little room.

Throwing open the windows, Joey greedily breathed in the good cold air, while her eyes surveyed the scene before her. She saw a church steeple on a not-too-distant hill, and far below in the valley, the town of Damüls, with its train station. Raising her eyes, she saw the never-ending peaks of the Austrian Alps. Joey gulped a few times when she reflected that it would be up there somewhere that her first brave attempts at skiing would take place, that is, if she didn't turn chicken first!

Next morning, refreshed from sleep and after eating a hearty breakfast, Joey and the others were introduced to their ski instructor. He was a native- born Austrian of slight build, charming manner, and the most fascinating accent that Joey had ever heard. One had to listen most attentively to understand all he said, but this only added flavour to the vacation.

It seemed he would be instructing them mornings and afternoons, each session lasting two hours. Great value for the reasonable price paid for the package! So here they were, being fitted for skis and boots in preparation for the first of many lessons. Joey had never had ski boots on before and was having a difficult time adjusting to their cumbersome size and weight, stumbling about and tripping over her own toes. She was quickly assured by a grinning Wolfgang, the ski instructor, that once the skis were attached to the boots, her problems would be over! She hoped sincerely his prediction would be right.

The next feat Joey had to attempt was carrying the skis. As there was little snow at their hotel's altitude, the ski lifts were not in operation, therefore, the party would have to hike the mountain in pursuit of it. Balancing the skis precariously on her shoulder, Joey at first struggled to find the position where they neither tipped forward nor back, but evenly distributed their weight. This would prevent the now-dangerous see-sawing motion and the possibility of clobbering those persons directly in front or behind her. Once the tilting act was worked out, she valiantly set off up the mountain with the others, following Wolfgang's lead.

Puffing and panting from the steep climb, the out-of-condition group rested awhile before the final assault to their playground in the sky. Seeing their spirits flagging, together with their bodies, Wolfgang pointed ahead to the fields of snow now visible to them. With renewed hope, they moved onward and upward to be soon rewarded by the crunching of snow beneath their feet and arrival at the beginner's slope.

'At last!' they cried together.

Helped by Wolfgang to unite boot and bindings, they found themselves now at the complete mercy of their skis. One young medical student in the group sneezed violently, which was enough to upset his balance, throwing him backwards into the snow, arms flailing, skis tilted irreverently to the heavens. Joey and the others roared laughing at his unexpected tumble, confident of their own abilities to remain upright. But before long, each had felt the sting of humiliation as they too became the subject of laughter, when without warning, their skis were bent on going in one direction, while their bodies insisted on another, ending in the inevitable tangle of skis, poles, arms, and legs heaped untidily on the snow.

The subtle meaning behind Wolfgang's prediction became all too plain to Joey later on that afternoon. While the problem of falling over her own toes had indeed been solved, she now found a new hazard in the ends of her skis, which became hopelessly crossed with each clumsy movement. Every pathetic attempt at uncrossing them only got her into deeper trouble as her legs began parting company. The gap between the skis at the back kept getting wider and wider, while the front ends remained locked, until she literally had achieved the splits. This hysterical position brought Joey's body into a full bow before she crashed face first into the snow.

Imprisoned by her skis, the bindings of which still held an iron grip on her boots, Joey was able only to yell and wait for the gallant Wolfgang to set her free.

'Some sense of humour he's got!' she mumbled, gulping a mouthful of snow in her anger.

The first day ended with the novices totally exhausted and their bodies bruised, each vowing never to put themselves in such danger again.

By the next morning, however, they were all ready to try once more after Wolfgang had convinced them that the only sure way of loosening up their now stiff and aching joints was to get them into motion as soon as possible.

As the group's confidence in their abilities increased, so did the injuries. Some became most daring in the feats they undertook. One rather portly, non-athletic member of the team, having finally mastered the trick of skiing straight down a gentle incline without falling, got carried away with enthusiasm one day by taking on a steeper hill. Face beaming, he pushed off in admirable posture for a beginner, all going well until about three-fourths of the way down, he realized to his horror that waiting for him at the bottom was a partly iced-over stream. Wolfgang had not yet shown the skiers how to stop or turn, so our friend, hurtling now as he was in a beeline for the rivulet, face pale with terror, chose the only method he knew of slowing down. Sitting abruptly on his bottom, he raised crystals of snow, as the brakes so to speak were applied, and then skidded the remainder of the way, stopping only a few feet short of the river!

Wolfgang spent many hours also instructing the novices in the art of traversing. Most did well, if for no other reason than for his words echoing clearly through the mountains, 'Uppah ski for-waaard.' It was the way he said this that intrigued everyone, so much so that at least it was always a gentle reminder in times of doubt as to which ski should be kept ahead of the other while performing this particular task, averting a possible accident.

One day, a show-off in the group, eager to demonstrate his prowess to the others, volunteered to traverse across the gentle slopes where everyone was assembled. With Wolfgang reminding him to keep 'Uppah ski for-waaard', he also showed superior balance by turning to look back over his shoulder at his comrades. All eyes followed this masterful one, even as they perceived he had travelled further than intended and was rapidly approaching a sharp drop-off to his course! He, unaware of his plight, continued on, till he most graciously disappeared from sight over the ravine. Suppressed laughter from the spectators broke out, while Wolfgang shamefacedly went to his aid.

For some time, Joey's ambition was the desire to ski fast down a hill, and go up one of those small snow mounds from where she could take off in a jump. She had witnessed many other skiers doing this, and it had looked relatively simple. So mustering her courage, she set off down the hill, scarf flying, knees bent, looking every bit the professional.

Upon approaching the mound with great speed, expecting her skis to go up to the summit for the take-off, she was completely stunned when the tips of the skis penetrated the small hill instead, instantly stopping their movement dead. Joey, however, continued her trajectory through the air, landing head buried in the snow. Luckily for her, the bindings this time let go, releasing her feet, preventing serious injury!

Not only did Joey have fun on the slopes, but splendid times were to be had too when the group returned to the hotel in the afternoons after a vigorous day's skiing. They were greeted by a roaring fire in the recreation room and Glüwein, a hot wine specialty of Austria and a delicious cold weather beverage. It was the time of day for relaxing, just chit-chatting and indoor games before dressing for dinner. Joey immensely enjoyed the camaraderie she found within the group. They laughed together easily about their mishaps on the ski runs, giving genuine support to each other. They were people from a variety of occupations who were easy-going and fun to be with. Joey found herself popular with the group due to her willingness to readily join in the many activities offered, such as charades, which never failed to have everyone doubled over with laughter, various card games, and Scrabble.

In the evenings, there was always something going on somewhere. For example, each hotel in the area would invite guests staying at neighbouring auberges to come and participate in dance evenings, or to be entertained by local people performing the Shoe-Platter, an Austrian folk dance.

It was at one such gathering that Joey met a good-looking man who asked her to dance. She had seen him before, at a distance, skiing expertly, and now she discovered his performance on the ballroom floor was equally good. He was the first man since Jan who had really caught her eye. Perhaps he would be the one to help her forget Jan. The end of the festivities that evening indeed seemed a long time off. Anyway, she continued to fantasize about this, until he asked to walk her back to her lodgings.

His name was Günther, a German, who was vacationing in another hotel not far from Joey's. The snow squeaked noisily underfoot as they made their way hand in hand along the country road, past the small white church that could be seen from Joey's window and where she had worshipped on Christmas Eve.

Arriving at her residence, Günther proffered his hand to bid her good night.

Hurriedly, lest she be robbed of the opportunity, Joey asked in a flustered tone, 'Won't you come in for a nightcap?'

Günther, obviously not expecting this invitation, stuttered, 'Oh... , ah... , I'd better not... it's getting late.'

'Oh?' Joey said disappointedly.

'No, really, Joey, I'd like to, but I have to be up early tomorrow.'

However, seeing the crestfallen expression on Joey's face, he softened and reluctantly agreed. 'Well, all right, but only for a moment.'

Joey was totally confused as to his changed attitude towards her. She tried hard to remember if she had done anything to warrant his resistance to her suggestion to come in, but found nothing.

There were no chairs in the room, so they sat cross-legged facing each other on the bed. Günther made no move to close the gap between them but said, 'How about the nightcap you promised?'

'What's wrong, don't you like me?'

'Yes, I like you,' came Günther's reply. 'Like we were this evening, dancing and having fun.'

'Then there is something wrong with me,' Joey interrupted.

'No, no, of course there isn't. Damn, I thought this could've been avoided.'

'What?'

'I'm a queer, that's what!'

Joey sat there stunned by this revelation, and in her ignorance, she didn't know whether she should say she was sorry or just what was appropriate. She was saved by embarrassment, however, by Günther's timely words.

'It's okay, Joey, I'm not offended by you or anything, you weren't to know. In fact, I put on such a good act of being a normal man that I not only fool everyone else, but I try to fool myself too. It's my mistake completely for trying to cover up.'

'You sound ashamed of what you are, Günther. Are you?'

'I guess I must be, or I wouldn't try to hide it, would I?'

'No, I guess not, but surely there's nothing to be ashamed of,' Joey said näively.

'Isn't there?' Günther sneered. 'You bet there's plenty. Listen, it's an intolerant world. Do you know what happens when you're found out?'

'No, I don't,' Joey feebly replied.

'To begin with, everyone thinks you're crazy, sick, you know—even afraid to be seen in your company, lest they're labelled too. It's worse than having leprosy, at least there's some hope given to lepers, but what hope do I have? Did you know that I could be gaoled and subjected to electric shocks? Worst of all, though, is when your own family disowns you, and they usually do.'

'How awful, Günther, but why?' 'Guilt, I expect.'

'Terrible! Did your family desert you?'

'Of course, don't want to see me. They're afraid I might corrupt other family members. Isn't that pathetic? Of course the whole thing makes me feel wretched and worthless, but there's nothing I can do about it.'

'I can see now why you try to keep it a secret, I would too.'

'Thank God, Joey, you're not queer, it's a lonely life.'

'I'm relieved we've talked about it. I understand better now how you feel.

This is the first time I've really talked to someone like you.'

'Well, it's mainly due to ignorance that we're made to feel like outcasts. After all, we're just the same as everyone else, except, we have a same gender orientation, that's all.'

'I feel privileged that you could share this with me, Günther, and I still like you a lot and want to be your friend.'

'You're sweet, Joey. And of course you can be.'

When Joey left Austria, she felt she had gained a valuable friend, for she and Günther shared an important secret, one she hoped he would not have to keep locked up forever. This experience was one Joey would never forget; it was new and revealing.

Chapter 26

Four months had passed since Joey's skiing holiday in Austria, and seven months with no word from Jan. She had become convinced she would never hear from him again and had given up writing.

Joey had dedicated herself fully to her teaching, even bringing as much work home as she could handle in order to keep busy. A few of her married colleagues invited her for dinner, but Joey felt their motivations were those of pity rather than anything else, and she started turning them down.

Amazingly, she began to prefer her own company to that of other people and their small talk. Even spending a Saturday night alone didn't bother her anymore. Joey now felt more selective and self-assured in choosing friends and confident about solving her problems without having someone else around. Of course she didn't entirely eliminate her need for other people, but the important change was that she had finally discovered she felt comfortable in her own skin.

Her mind relatively calm, having put Jan and even the abortion to the back of her mind, Joey wondered if this then wasn't the perfect situation. No petty jealousies to keep her constantly on edge, no conflict, no one else to worry about. It might be a cop-out, but it was a welcome refuge for now, and Joey intended to enjoy the serenity this protective shell afforded her.

The letter, bearing a Swedish postmark and in Jan's handwriting, was delivered one Saturday morning. Joey stared at it with disbelief. After all this time, he chose to remind her that he was still around. How predictable he was. Jan would give her sufficient time to pursue her life alone, only to reappear and commence the vicious circle once more.

'Well, that won't happen again', Joey muttered to herself, 'not this time.'

This, however, was vowed before reading Jan's endearing letter, which softened her heart considerably, as she proceeded to read the following:

April 1958

My Darling,

I beg you to forgive me for not writing you before. I am desolate without you—it's like you were dead! I need you, Joey, more than you believe. I've also thought a lot about marriage while we've been apart. I want to marry you and settle down with a home somewhere and have kids. God, I hope I'm not too late!

I left France shortly after you did. I couldn't continue to live where memories of you haunted me in every place we'd been together.

As you can see, Joey, from the envelope, I'm back in Stockholm and have found myself a job. This will show you the extent of my sincerity in wanting to settle down. In any case, I'd like you to come to Sweden and see for yourself. Please consider my proposal of marriage, won't you?

My love always,
Jan

Joey's eyes were misty with tears as she read his letter. The rest dealt with news of his family, emphasising that his mother, sister Barbro, and her young son, who all lived together, were looking forward to meeting her. She wondered at his sincerity. Could he have changed so much? Was he genuinely tired of his gypsy existence?

The answers lay with Jan in Sweden, and the only way to know would be to go there and find out. After all, they had broken up because of his unwillingness to settle down. If indeed he was now ready to make honourable commitments, why shouldn't she go, she reasoned, and see if he would carry them through. She loved him as she always had, in spite of her bittersweet feelings. In any case, it was the first time he had mentioned marriage in these terms, and that's what she ultimately wanted.

Joey replied to Jan, but with two conditions. The first would depend on her success at obtaining work, for at no cost would she forego her independence. The second hinged on the understanding that they would live separately until they married. Joey had fallen into the live-together trap before and did not wish to repeat it. They could test their feelings for each other before any final step was made. Satisfied with her answer, Joey mailed the letter.

Chapter 27

The meeting at the train station had been a tender one. Joey had gazed lovingly at Jan's face and then she was swept up in his arms. They stayed together embracing, kissing, and crying tears of joy until a voice from behind brought them to attention. With arms outstretched in welcome, Jan's sister said warmly, 'Hello, you must be Joey, I'm Barbro. Glad you've come to our country', and then with a warm smile, turned and gave her brother a hug, he responding by planting a kiss on her forehead.

'You didn't tell me she was so pretty, Jan.'

'I wanted you to see for yourself.'

Joey thought Barbro was quite beautiful. Blond shoulder-length hair, the bluest of blue eyes fringed with long eyelashes setting off an ivory complexion. She was somewhat blown away by her beauty before finding her voice and stammering.

'Thanks, er, thank you, Barbro, for coming to meet me. I feel quite special.'

'Well, there's someone else who's dying to meet you too,' she said, and taking Joey by the hand, with Jan in tow, they were led to the station's waiting room. Barbro stopped in front of an elegantly dressed and coiffed middle-aged lady and announced, 'This is our mother.' Mrs Ekberg rose quickly to her feet to greet Joey with a warm hug.

'I'm so happy to meet you, Mrs Ekberg', said Joey, 'and I trust that we'll get to see a lot more of each other.'

'Yes, dear, I'll make sure of that.'

'And so will I,' put in Barbro. 'We'd like you to think of us as family.'

Turning to her son, Mrs Eckberg said in a no-nonsense voice, 'You will treat her right or you'll have me to answer to.'

Jan looked sheepish at this remark but nodded his head in recognition.

The first disappointment in this latest reunion came when Joey arrived at her new lodgings. Jan had gone back on his word and found a room in a guesthouse in which he intended they cohabit!

Infuriated by Jan's blatant disregard of her wishes, Joey felt like leaving Sweden on the next train. Unfortunately, she had once more been the pawn in this move and had nothing to return to in England. In frustration over this sudden change to her safe scheme, she blurted out, 'I thought we agreed to living separately until after marriage?'

'So we did, but I couldn't imagine you were serious, Joey—that's so old- fashioned.'

'Old-fashioned or not, that's the way I want it, Jan. God, do you ever take anything I say seriously?'

'You just don't know what's best for you, that's all.'

'Please let's not start that nonsense again. If anyone knows what I want, it's certainly me.'

'I'm not sure about that at all. We agreed to a testing of our feelings, didn't we, and there's no better way than this. Maybe we're no longer compatible in bed.' Of course Joey knew it was impossible to argue with him. She certainly didn't want a fight so soon after her arrival.

Incompatibility in their sexual relations proved no problem, but had served him as an excuse to con his way back into Joey's bed. She took a much more mature approach this time by having herself fitted with a diaphragm. She would definitely take charge of her body, no longer recklessly leaving results to fate. She also secretly planned to find a place of her own in order to take a firm stand with Jan.

When Joey received encouragement and support from Barbro, who helped her find a bedsit, she immediately packed for the move, leaving a startled and angry Jan.

'You'll regret this, Joey!'

'I don't think so. I hope you'll respect my wishes in the future, if there's to be one. Show me you really love me and want to settle down,' Joey called to him over her shoulder as she closed the door behind her and left.

Joey had managed to obtain a job in an international school in Stockholm, beginning September 1958, which primarily served the needs of the diplomatic community. The fascinating part of her work here was teaching English to children from practically every ethnic and racial background.

She taught 6-year-olds and delighted in their progress when, after only three months, they not only conversed in English, but also wrote well too. Of course the perfect opportunity for goofing off was always present. A student need just plead a lack of understanding to be let off with a simpler task. One little boy named Aklilu, from Ghana, cute and mischievous, with eyes large enough to melt the devil's soul, had become quite adroit at this game and found himself foiled one day when he tried his familiar ploy.

'Me no understand,' he said ever so innocently.

'You understand all right, Aklilu,' came Joey's firm reply and, with a gentle tap on his bottom, sent him smartly back to his lessons, where he again worked like a little Trojan!

Jan laboured at clerical jobs, which of course he hated, but for someone with such a history of unreliability, it was not surprising that he could find nothing better to do, not even in his own country. He would stick to the work for maybe a month or two, then quit and stay at home to recuperate from the experience.

Jan contacted Joey every day and they saw each other at weekends, when he would relay to her the bad news about his job. Joey remained steadfast, saying, 'You're behaving like a spoiled brat.'

'I deny that! The mundane tasks I perform really make me psychologically sick and then I just can't face another day.'

While the topic of how Jan spent his workless days had never been broached by Joey, Jan had given the impression that each day was spent in serious pursuit of a worthwhile career. This illusion came to an abrupt end one day, when Joey had offered to pick up Jan's one and only suit to take to the dry-cleaner's. Normally she would never have gone through his pockets, but on this occasion felt the search was warranted. To her astonishment, she found in his jacket a wad of notes, a substantial sum of money. She flicked them through her fingers in disbelief, wondering how he had come by this windfall. Her curiosity gave way to anger when she felt she'd been taken for a ride.

She was so incensed at that moment that if Jan had been present, she would have torn him apart. When he telephoned her next, she could not wait to lash out at him.

'So you've been hiding money from me, have you?' 'Yes, as a matter of fact,' came his cool reply.

Taken aback by his frank admission, Joey was suddenly dumbstruck. 'Well', he added, 'aren't you dying to know where it came from?' Finding her tongue once more, Joey stammered, 'Y-yess.'

'As a matter of fact, I've been saving it.' 'From what?' asked Joey.

'The money you'd been giving me every week.' 'But I thought you were using that to look for a job.' 'Well, I have, but I haven't been looking every day.'

'I thought you had. What a cad you are, Jan. How could you let me struggle with the budgeting when you had that money?'

'I was going to surprise you.' 'When?'

'For your birthday, but that's all spoiled now,' Jan said disappointedly. 'Oh I'm sorry, I didn't mean to. I found the money by accident.'

'Forget it, Joey, but next time don't be so ready to jump to conclusions.' The subject was closed, with Jan the victor. It was nearly always like this, she feeling guilty for something she hadn't done, except maybe to question his integrity. Why she had this growing feeling of distrust for him was not quite clear, nor the nagging belief that he was not always telling her the truth. In any case, she had no proof of any shenanigans on his part and would have to contain her suspicions.

Chapter 28

Unlike France, in Sweden Joey had been able to form a very close bond of friendship with Jan's sister Barbro, who was a few years older than herself. She was a most independent woman, and one to whom Joey could relate very well.

Barbro was an exact opposite of Jan. She was reliable and responsible in her work and in caring for her son. This situation was the result of an ill- fated love affair with a married man. Barbro had been very young and innocent when she met him by chance in a cafe too. He had been debonair and charming, she told Joey, and before she knew what was happening, they had set up house together. He, of course, had assured her from the beginning of his love and that he would marry her if only his wife would consent to a divorce. His wife never did and Barbro ended the affair.

Joey was becoming more and more amazed at the increasing number of love affairs and marriages that she saw ending disastrously. Where, she wondered, were those happy people like Bob and Amy who had once been the norm? Everyone seemed to be experiencing some kind of heartbreak.

Joey hadn't been prepared for this at all in her growing up. For that matter, she didn't know of anyone else who had either. She was saddened and disappointed that love, marriage, and living happily ever after was not always the ideal union her parents had enjoyed.

Romance seemed to be the elusive quality women wanted in their relationships with men, while the males on the other hand appeared to need mothers. Neither sex adequately lives up to the expectations of the other, destroying fantasies and ultimately love, which to Joey was nothing more than sexual attraction. That would explain the reason for so many break- ups, for once the desires burned lower, there was nothing left.

These reflections about love were inspired by Barbro's predicament primarily, but Joey's position was shaky enough. For what, if anything, lay beneath the surface of this off again, on again affair with Jan? What would be left when she woke to find the stars no longer in her eyes? At the moment when Joey was not playing games with herself, she knew there wouldn't be much.

After all, she recognized they had few common interests with which to form a strong bond in later years. Their backgrounds were totally different in every aspect—ethnically and religiously. Heaven knows they'd had numerous fights over this: she was a believer, and he was an atheist!

Even their political views were in discord. Joey didn't even know she had an opinion on this subject, until one day she made a remark concerning army deserters. She learned from this that Jan had been a draft evader, having successfully absconded to Switzerland, avoiding conscription in his own land.

Joey had thought this a most cowardly and unpatriotic act, and her respect for him had dwindled.

She could understand now how arranged marriages usually lasted so much better. Without romance, but based on mutual respect and interest. Surely there was no better foundation.

Joey wondered how much respect was left between her and Jan. How complex everything became if you sat down and analysed it, but how much better life would ultimately be if you did. Of course youth would never take this wiser path, running headlong as they did wherever the heart led. Why, she herself had been impetuous too, only stopping to weigh the situation at this late stage after first being severely stung.

Jan's inability to stay at a job for any length of time, his moodiness, leaving Joey as he did for days at a time without contacting her, left little reason for respect. His promises of marriage were never fulfilled, but brushed aside with petty excuses. At best she was now certain he was definitely emotionally immature, he really couldn't cope with his own feelings let alone respond to her needs. He had obviously missed something in his growing up and was still learning about himself. Maybe being raised by a mother alone had led to his present dilemma, his parents having divorced while he was still quite young. Yet Barbro seemed to have turned out as a well-balanced person.

The awareness she now had concerning Jan's immaturity gave Joey a new perspective on marriage, or at least where he was concerned. It was the first time since knowing Jan that she thought she was not so keen on the idea anymore. She was beginning to realize that the great interest and excitement she felt with him was most probably due to his foreignness. His accent alone was enough to put her in a spin, and somehow it was chic, or so she had thought, to date someone so completely different from one's self in spite of their differences. Joey could now see that with the blend of Jan's immaturity and her fiercely independent spirit, that their path of matrimony would be rocky at best.

In spite of all her level-headed deductions, Joey was still not prepared to dismiss their association lightly, as if it hadn't taken place, nor to state categorically that her feelings for Jan were not those of love. She had assumed that because of the care and concern she had felt for Jan, as she had for no other person, that indeed it must be love.

Chapter 29

Barbro and Joey were jammed between other perspiring bodies in a second-class carriage of the Continental Flyer, after leaving Barbro's boy in the loving care of his grandma. This old steam train was bound for Italy, and all along its route, from the northernmost tip of Scandinavia, it had swept up hordes of holiday-crazed tourists. It was August in Europe, and this meant that everyone was heading for somewhere—anywhere—as long as it was not home. Joey had never seen such madness! The roads were jammed with motorists, airports groaned with the unceasing roar of plane engines, while pushing and shoving crowds overflowed their terminals. Barbro, like her fellow Europeans, had been unable to choose another time to travel, as her company had closed its doors for a month without a thought that any other time might make more sense. Joey had no choice in the matter if she wished to holiday with Barbro.

The compartment in which they were sandwiched had gradually swelled with people the further south they got. Those unfortunates, who were the latest additions to the train, found themselves occupying the corridors.

Everywhere though, even amid the crush of humanity, there was a picnic atmosphere. Wine bottles and flasks could be seen all round, while large sausages and cheese were drawn from sacks, to be eventually wedged between crusts of Italian bread. With fanfares of hand waving in accompaniment to excited chatter, everyone by now was sharing food with their neighbour. This was especially noticeable from the Italian tourists, who seemed to outdo their fellow travellers, both in loudness and gesture. Joey was at a loss to understand why these people had troubled to bring food and drink along with them when they could easily have purchased the same from vendors at any of the numerous stations at which they stopped. She, for one, wouldn't have bothered to carry it. Barbro explained it was a throwback to earlier times. Travelling was not only hazardous then but lengthy, and refreshments couldn't be bought readily along the way. This also gave a man his independence and security. The custom continued, or at least with some races it had. Joey thought that the tasteless, overpriced food of the refreshment stands was probably the modern-day reason for keeping alive these habits, especially among the nationalities boasting more refined palates.

Sleeping upright had never come easily for Joey. Now it was made more difficult by lack of space and frequent stops during the night. These on their own would not have been too bad, but accompanied by screeching brakes, followed soon after by rattles and bangs as the rest of the train caught up and finally came to a jerking stop, shaking even the deepest of sleepers from their slumber, proved too much. On one occasion, when Joey had managed to nod off, she had been woken by a fellow traveller politely asking her to remove her feet from his lap as this was really too uncomfortable. She also learned that sleep was impossible during the night if you crossed into different countries. No matter what the hour, an army of border guards and inspectors swarmed onto the train.

No one was spared as they hunted every nook and cranny to check the validity of the passports of all aboard this pleasure train. Even in the elite first-class carriages, doors were thrown open and the inhabitants roused. Then as swiftly and abruptly as they had arrived, they vanished, and the train rolled on again, clanging its way closer to each traveller's destination.

Rimini, Italy, came not before time as far as Joey and Barbro were concerned, for they felt their bodies couldn't have taken one more sleepless night. Bleary-eyed and without any hotel reservations, the two made their way to an information desk at the station. In a few minutes, they learned there were no hotel vacancies left in Rimini. Of course, they had speculated on this possibility, and yet had done nothing about it, assuming that something would turn up. Joey especially hated to book for anything ahead of time, always preferring to trust to good fortune.

Lady Luck smiled on them, however, for they were offered a small cottage they could rent. This would be even better they thought, for they could prepare their own meals and save money. The catch to the proposition was that the house was not in Rimini proper, but farther north along the coast. Without transportation, except for an occasional bus, this would be a nuisance if they wished to come to town for entertainment. Joey was quick to point out to Barbro the possibility of hitch-hiking and, as she now considered herself almost an expert in this area, even offered to show her the finer points.

Stationed with their suitcases beside them, Joey, full of self-confidence, initiated the thumb-raising technique. Before long, a number of motorists had blocked the road to stop and stare at these pretty girls. Musical horns played and the cars now caused a minor traffic jam. Suddenly over this melodious gathering, the girls detected a police siren. Miraculously the traffic dissipated as the flashing lights on the officers' auto came into view. Pulling up, these lawmen looked both women up and down, apparently liked what they saw, and personally drove them to their cottage, whereupon they left the two with the warning not to trust Italian men!

Joey was determined to enjoy this holiday to the hilt, especially as Jan had not approved of her going without him. He even went as far as saying that she'd be miserable minus his company. So it was not surprising that bright and early the next morning, Joey and Barbro were frolicking on the beach. The first attention-getters were heads—lots of heads sticking up out of the sand. Joey smiled at the spectacle, having only witnessed children playing this silly game before, and these heads most definitely belonged to adults!

'What do you suppose they're doing that for?' asked Joey.

'Doing what?' came Barbro's surprised reply.

'Look over there, see all those heads.'

'Oh, you mean the people who are buried?' 'That's weird. What are they doing, Barbro?'

'You're not serious, Joey, you mean you really don't know?' 'I swear.'

'Very good for easing the pain of arthritis, I believe.' 'What does?'

'Being buried in the warm sand.' 'Hmm, makes good sense, I guess.'

They enjoyed the tepid waters of the Adriatic, then Joey and Barbro headed for a delightful sidewalk cafe for lunch. The friendliness of these places had always pleased Joey, together with the superb food at moderate prices, to say nothing of the excellent view of the passing parade. The colourful umbrellas shading the chequered tablecloths, lush ripe fruit immersed in bowls of cool water, Italian style, with the inevitable bottle of Chianti, indeed whet the appetite.

Sitting back, each enjoying her wine, who should the two girls see getting off their Vespas and heading for their table? The two policemen who had taken them to their cottage the night before! They looked very different in swim trunks, but still recognizable. Both girls automatically looked them up and down, appraising their muscular physiques, great tans, and sleeked- back hair. 'He's nice, the one on the left,' said Joey quietly.

'You can have him,' Barbro just managed to whisper before the two men reached their table.

'Bon giorno, come va?' said Joey's choice. 'Bon giorno, buono,' the girls responded.

'If you've finished lunch, would you like to come for a ride with us to Rimini?' said the other off-duty policeman in good English.

'I don't think we should. How about you, Barbro?'

'I agree, especially as they told us not to trust Italian men.'

'We didn't mean us,' Joey's choice quipped back.

'You're Italian men, aren't you?' Barbro said confidently.

'We've agreed that we won't go with you for a ride, but how about joining us for a drink?' put in Joey.

'Ebbene,' the men replied in unison.

After refreshments, however, the girls felt more at ease with the men and finally agreed to the ride, which secretly they wanted to do since they'd seen Audrey Hepburn in *Roman Holiday*.

It was a hair-raising experience that ensued, manoeuvring at an alarming rate through the traffic. No one, it seemed, bothered with any road rules whatsoever, each intent on getting wherever he was going, by the fastest, shortest route possible. To the surprise of the two girls, their escorts suddenly came to a lurching stop just outside Rimini's city limits and began donning shirts and pants.

'Why are you doing that now?' asked Joey curiously.

'We could be fined,' replied Giorgio, her driver. 'For what, just driving in bathing suits?'

'Yes, we have a law against any form of nakedness,' Lorenzo, the other one, said.

'What difference does it make for a man to have a bare top?' teased Joey. 'Besides you're the police anyway, who's going to fine you?'

'Don't worry about that, we'd be booked too, the law's the law,' said Giorgio.

'Strange custom,' Joey said, shaking her head.

They continued on into town in silence, finally coming to a halt in the city's main square. The boys then took them sightseeing on foot, pointing out historical buildings, which to Joey should have been all of them, if for no other reason than their sheer age. These buildings had been built before Australia had even been discovered!

They danced till sunrise in a night club in Rimini, then the foursome returned to the cottage carrying a bottle of wine to finish their party. Italians are hot-blooded, as Joey knew so well from her hitch-hiking trip. This time she was better prepared and the girls agreed they would say arrividerci to their boys after one drink each. They got no opposition from them, and all agreed they'd had a good time.

Before retiring for the night, the girls pondered the friendliness shown by the men. In fact this seemed a trait of the people of Southern Europe, and they wondered if the temperament were not synonymous with climate. It certainly was a sunny land, this Italy, and its natives were happy, warm, and amorous. In contrast, Sweden, the land of the midnight sun, was formal and its people more serious-minded or so it seemed. In any case, Joey knew her vacation in this sun-drenched land would be fun with these compassionate Italians.

Chapter 30

Looking forward to the prospect of seeing Jan again, Joey and Barbro sprinted, with suitcases, the short distance from the train station to Barbro's apartment where they had arranged to meet Jan. However, once inside and finding the place empty, Joey's enthusiasm quickly turned to bitter disappointment. At first she thought he may have been unsure of the time she was arriving, even though she had taken great pains to spell this out to him in her letters. Tears rolled down her cheeks and she sought solace from Barbro. She sensed that his no-show this time was of a more serious nature. 'I don't know what to say, Joey, except that I think you're crazy to put up with him, even though he's my brother. I know I wouldn't!'

'Come on, Barbro, you know better than to say that. What did you do for that man who wouldn't divorce for you?'

'You're wrong, Joey, he always treated me right. He never walked all over me like you allow Jan to do with you.'

'No, but he finally left you pregnant.'

'I still say he was very good to me while we were together.'

'The undying loyalty of women. When are you going to admit he was just using you, Barbro? After all, he was a married man.'

'I really don't feel he was as bad as you seem to think.'

'Fooling around with you when he was already married isn't bad?'

'I loved him, and enjoyed the times we had together. You know, Joey, he made me feel I was the only one. I'll always have the memories of those good times.'

'And that's enough? I don't just want memories, I think I deserve something tangible! It's true, Barbro, I've put up with a lot from Jan. Funny how our preferences are so totally different. I guess that's our backgrounds. I wouldn't want to share my man with anyone else,' Joey said firmly.

'Surely, Joey, it's better to have something for some of the time than nothing all of the time.'

'Yes, when you put it like that, but why can't I have all, all of the time, Barbro?'

'That would be wonderful, but I don't think possible.'

'That's my ideal, and I have no intention of abandoning it yet,' Joey retorted.

'I'm happy for you, and I hope you find what you're looking for, but how come you think you'll find that Utopia with Jan? You've been through enough already to know life with him is uncertain.'

'Maybe, Barbro, I'm fooling myself with the hope that everything will turn out okay in the end.'

What Barbro was saying was pretty much like her own thoughts on arranged marriages. That is to say that common interests and general compatibility were really what kept a marriage together ultimately, not sex as many young people so ignorantly believed. Of course the ideal was the blend of the two. How fortunate the couples were who had this magic combination. Joey wondered if her own parents would fit this idealistic category, happy as they were in each other's company.

With the mystery of Jan's disappearance still gnawing at her, Joey late that evening boarded a bus for home. She took a seat to the rear and leaned her head against the window. Staring out into the night, she watched the twinkling lights of the shops as the bus rumbled along the cobbled roadway. As the bus stopped to pick up passengers, Joey's attention was diverted to the crowds pouring out from a movie house, and there amongst them she spotted Jan. He was not alone, for his arm encircled a pretty blonde, who held his attention in animated conversation.

At first Joey wanted to pound on the window to get his attention away from this female and let him know that she had seen. Anger rose in her breast at the sight of her man touching another woman. Her feelings of possessiveness came to the fore, and jumping from her seat, she made her way to the exit. The bus at that moment was thrown into gear by the driver, and it leaped away from the curb to continue on its way.

In Joey's eyes, Jan had been unfaithful, and from this night on, her actions would be clear cut. She would no longer have anything more to do with him. This had put the lid on the affair. In spite of what Barbro had said, she could not nor would she tolerate it. No matter how he might plead for forgiveness in the future, she would never give in to him again. There was absolutely no way she could share Jan with other women. She'd had this inkling all along that their love would not survive. Even now the idea of leaving Jan forever was unreal, yet she knew it would come—had to come. She would go home at last to Australia.

Jan turned up again after a few weeks, as was to be expected. He was filled with his usual self-confidence that Joey would forgive everything, but was astonished to find her, if anything, quite cold.

'Come on, Joey, let's forgive and forget.' 'Forgive what?'

'Well, aren't you mad at me for going off?'

'Hurt and disappointed would probably describe my feelings best right now,' answered Joey.

'Don't get dramatic—it's not the first time, you've lived through it.'

'Yes, like a damn fool I did, but then I didn't know there was another woman. I believed your lies.'

'Who's been filling your head with that nonsense?' Jan said calmly. 'You're denying it?' said Joey unbelievingly.

'Of course! There's no other woman but you, never has been, and never will be. I'll bet that sister of mine's been talking to you, that's what!'

'Liar!' Joey screamed. 'I saw you with my own eyes.' 'You must have been seeing things, I swear.'

'You were with a blonde coming out of the movies, I saw you from the bus.'

'Nonsense, must've been someone who looked like me—you're mistaken.'

'Are you trying to tell me I'm crazy or something? God, Jan, I'd know you anywhere. You're even too much of a coward to admit you've been caught, how I despise that.'

'You're in no mood to reason with I can see—I'll be back some other time.'

'I'd like the door key before you go,' Joey said firmly.

'Sure, take it,' Jan yelled, tossing it on the floor.

Later that day, Joey instructed the landlady that she would not be at home anymore to receive Jan, nor to talk with him on the phone in the event he should call. Her mind was fully made up about returning to Australia for Christmas.

Joey sorted out her diary this time to record the pain she felt. Jan's infidelity had been devastating, but she knew that writing down her thoughts would help to release pent-up feelings. This channel had become her most trusted earpiece and confidante in which she could bare her very soul. The words she penned flowed as if from her veins into the following poem:

August 1959

Lovers

He touched my life,
I wept with joy.
Fulfillment reached,
Happiness come.
We loved—Hearts rang,
Our hands entwined.
Promises made,
The future's bright.

SHE passed his way,
I am sad,
Forsaken now
For another.
Yesterday's gone,
Paradise lost.
I weep still,
For my lover.

J.McP.

Chapter 31

Joey knew she was truly home in Cardellum when the car driven by her father swung onto the all-too-familiar dirt road, leaving the main highway behind masked in a veil of swirling dust. Time had preserved its ruts and holes, it seemed, for her homecoming. The kookaburra's laugh still rang from the lofty gum trees. It was as if Joey had awakened from a long, long sleep, to find nothing changed, or at least Nature had remained intact in this sleepy corner of the world. Joey was glad that her birthplace had been spared the axe's blow, and the inevitable developers that followed in the wake of man's destruction of the countryside. She had already seen too much of this in other countries, but secretly knew that Nature would win in the end, enduring long after man to reclaim the earth.

Joey was shocked by the toll that time had taken on her parents, especially her mother. Time had not been kind. The initial shock had come when she saw them at the airport. Neither one was as sprightly as she had remembered, and her mother's hair had greyed. The wrinkles on her once- velvety skin now gave a more weathered appearance. This was a most hurtful sight to Joey, for like any other child, she had taken her mother's immortality for granted. To be faced so harshly with the reality that she was getting old and would not always be there to render comfort stabbed at her heart, causing Joey to embrace her mother with a special tenderness she had not previously shown. The two had remained locked in each other's arms weeping.

Pangs of guilt tore at Joey's conscience, as she thought of the years she had deprived her parents of her presence and help, while she had selfishly sought to satisfy her own needs. She could not recapture those years, but would try to make up for them as best she could.

Both her brothers had changed radically, especially Ken, who had been a mere schoolboy when she had left on her adventures. He was almost unrecognisable. Sometimes she would find a hint of his former self by the way he curled his lip when he smiled, or in an all-too-familiar glimmer that came into his eyes when he told a story. Piece by piece Joey matched these expressions, until his face came into full focus, and in the man's countenance, she found her brother's.

While the land and its soil had stood still, nothing else on this trip into her past had. She had set out one morning soon after her arrival in search of her old haunts and a touch of nostalgia. Her bicycle, squeaky with rust from lack of use, carried her as it had always done, over the bumpy road to the corner shop to obtain the school's keys from the proprietor. He had been nominated to look after them until the fate of the school was determined. The store was smaller than she had remembered it, and certainly in much worse condition. Its walls were pockmarked with cracks and holes, and it was apparent it had fallen victim to dry rot. The front steps where the teenagers had gathered like clockwork now supported two lazy old dogs snoozing in the sun.

Joey pedalled on to the old schoolhouse. Two years after she had left Australia, this building had joined the ranks of the obsolete, abandoned for the great, sophisticated schools, which comprised the centralised school district. The few children left in Cardellum, together with others from outlying areas, were bussed many miles each day to these well-equipped places of learning. The era of the one-teacher school was doomed, and as a teacher, Joey was greatly saddened. Nothing could ever replace the rapport experienced between teacher and child, nor the concern and caring the students had for each other. Surely that was the perfect environment for learning.

Gingerly she unlocked the school door, afraid lest her memories of this cherished place would not be the same. To her delight, everything remained as Paul Duke, the last head teacher, must have left it, save for the dust, spread like a thin film over the desks. Joey made her way to a seat and sat among the ghosts of her past. They were all there, her old classmates, bubbling with mischievous excitement, as they had so long ago, especially when the teacher's attention had been riveted to the blackboard. She spotted the corner that she had graced more than once for insupportable behaviour. Her fingers lovingly encircled the old inkwell, now dried up, which once was filled to the brim. After generations of voices and laughter, now stilled forever by this closing, the silence was eerie.

Joey's memories of this place had been mainly happy ones, and the site of the thought-provoking discussion she'd had with Mr Duke concerning a career. She sat for a long time basking in her dreams and thinking how sad it was to have lost the past and one's youth, but also how wonderful to be able, on occasion, to relive them. She knew at that moment that her future would be in the classroom where she had never been disappointed. But Cardellum had no future for her, so where would teaching take her next?

The change in customs had come about by the gradual shift of the younger people to the cities for higher education and, finally, work. This generation was no longer satisfied to toil on the land for little recompense, as the ones before them had. Now in the late fifties, these youngsters were more sophisticated, influenced a great deal by television.

Most of the older residents had continued their resistance to electricity, still mainly due to the expense, the same way they had when Joey was growing up and, as a result, had no television. Luckier people with their own generators did, and this afforded them the only form of entertainment, apart from church-related activities within the confines of the village itself.

The children found this 'new-fangled box', as the oldies called the television sets, if not at home, at school. They had finally replaced the educational radio broadcasts that had educated Joey. From these they acquired more expensive tastes by way of commercials telling the populace, young and old, what they needed. University students clamoured for cars, where bicycles had once sufficed. Fashion-conscience teenagers emerged, donning Sunday's clothes on weekdays. No wonder many didn't want the land their forebears had worked with such diligence. Even Joey's brothers had chosen other occupations.

Tom taught at an agricultural college, and Ken had become a veterinarian, still living in Cardellum but travelling to nearby towns. Joey guessed he too would leave home though, if he married.

It was obvious that Cardellum had become a no-growth village. Worse still, it looked as if it were headed for extinction, a ghost town in the making. With the exodus of the young, the old were left farming until death overtook them, leaving the farms to fall to neglect. Joey had noticed many farms in this state as she pedalled the length and breadth of the hamlet.

Old Ned, dead now for some years, had left his legacy to the town, nothing but his crumbled shack and his faithful boat lying beached as he had left it, its hull encrusted with the remains of barnacles.

Decay was everywhere, and Joey worried about the future of her parents. Her father who had always been able to supplement his income as a guide to sport fishermen now found that many bypassed Cardellum in favour of larger seaside towns. These could boast better boats and equipment and take their customers farther out to sea to land prized catches.

Little wonder then that Nature had been spared here—the town was dying! Her first joyous feelings at seeing the countryside preserved were now saddened as she realized why. Nobody wanted to live in Cardellum, because it lacked the excitement and amenities that television had told them they needed in order to be happy!

Joey was upset by what she saw, for this was the last thing she had expected would happen to this peaceful place. She had always believed her home and roots to be secure. It was a shame that this town that had always boasted such kinship now was seeing the end of an era.

Yet in fact, Joey knew she certainly had not contributed much to the preservation of her community, or its lifestyle, having herself left to pursue a career elsewhere. She could not lay blame on the young, for just doing what she had been guilty of before. At that time, though, Cardellum had shown no signs of its imminent death, she reasoned, or she would have stayed.

The disappointment at finding her hometown in such a decline made Joey all the more remorseful at having left it. Not that she could have prevented its demise even if she had remained. This was no more than a sign of the times, but made more hurtful for her, because unlike the other residents, she had been unable to suddenly accept the inevitability of change. Cruelly, Joey's fond memories of her birthplace had been smashed in an instant on her return, leaving her no chance to adapt to this new reality surrounding her.

Chapter 32

Seated before her bedroom mirror, Joey gazed intently at her image, pondering her life to date. It was late evening, and the warm glow given off by the kerosene lamp played uncanny tricks with her reflection. Strange how this glass could present her many faces, with such clarity and keen focus as if a film was being unreeled. Interesting, too, the parade of events that had been her life so far.

Now the glass captured the innocent, näive child skipping across the paddocks with a carefree heart. Looking, questioning, learning. Everything at that tender age is an adventure, looked upon with wide-eyed wonderment and exuberance. No evil thoughts to fester the soul, no doubts to cloud the horizon, rather a trusting love and spontaneity to embrace the world. Deception has not been learned, the tongue untainted by falsehoods. A time in one's life that passes before having really been savoured. Sad thought, but true nonetheless. Joey had been that little girl with the smiling face and the happy childhood, which now was gone, but had left its imprint on her character, as everything along life's path will do, making each person unique.

The burning wick in the lamp, flicked by a slight breeze, cast a different light across the mirror, and Joey cringed to see the awkward teenager gawking back. How self-conscious and unsure she had been, ashamed of her pimply face, and much too coy to look the boys in the eye. The threshold of adulthood, it seems, is a difficult time for most people—too many doubts, too many choices, pressures, and decisions, overwhelming in their vastness, impossible to handle. Demands pouring in from parents and school, and tucked away inside the soul, that oh so wonderful, inexplicable feeling when the opposite sex comes close. All at once, parents are overly concerned about your whereabouts, who you're with, and when you'll be back.

Joey's thoughts turned to Benny Bradford, her childhood sweetheart. The first boy to give her that goose-pimply feeling. What an innocent affair is a first love; why, just to hold hands had been a big thrill. Eventually though they had progressed to more daring acts, such as kissing, but only through the use of props that aided them over their shyness. In this particular case, cards were used. Joey's brother Tom had introduced them to this wicked game, explaining to Benny the pleasures to be found in this sport. Tom's payment for such teaching was usually a much-coveted football or racket, fishing pole, or desired object he had seen Benny with. The idea of the game was for the boy to cut the pack of playing cards in half, having first shuffled them well. He would then proceed to present the upturned card to the girl. The process would be repeated, he taking the next card. Whoever had the highest number would score with a kiss. The two were delighted with the rules, for whichever way their cards turned up, they were winners.

Unfortunately, deceit and lies creep into one's life by the teens, and Joey gasped a little as a shadow hovered over her mirrored countenance, throwing the once-clear reflection slightly out of focus. The innocence of her earlier years was lost forever in this distortion.

The scene changed again, and Joey blinked with disbelief at what appeared to be her mother's face peering back at her, but it was gone in an instant. There she perceived herself just grown. No more than a fledgling woman, ready and poised to leave the nest, but not sure of the right moment to take flight. Still very much her parents' child. A part of their thoughts, beliefs, morals, and teachings. Afraid to let go, to emerge alone from her shell. Then a loving nudge and push from family to launch her on her solo flight. Once alone, Joey began to lay her plans, make decisions, and take on responsibilities. Security of her home and loved ones at this stage of her development, however, was only a telephone call away, with any needed reassurance readily and willingly given.

Spellbound now by the mirror, Joey's gaze was riveted on her woman of yesterday. Stumbling and fearful, a novice in the game of life. Ignorant of the world outside her own, its peoples, customs, languages, and morals. The religions she had never heard about and poverty not dreamed about. Beggars, and vice never before seen, and opinions on these subjects formed and reformed until a point of view could be reached. Tolerance of others different from herself severely put to the test, where there had been no need before. Compassion aroused for those less fortunate due to a lopsided economic world.

Joey's warm heart and light spirit at this time of her life were wide open to love and affection, but also vulnerable to hurt and suffering. Cherished dreams of a happy future were securely embedded in her mind. Evil was still a foreign word, and loosening of morals not considered. Her brow was slightly furrowed, and her eyes alert with disbelief at sights of ugliness not previously witnessed. Joey's mouth, always so ready to smile, had by now taken an almost imperceptible, but permanent downward curve, in sympathy for the hopelessness that disease and poverty had brought to millions of people.

A sadder, older mien with eyes deep in secrets now looked back at Joey. Her today face. As she studied it with some remorse, for the loss of the younger, happier expression of bygone days, she pondered the living she had done, showing itself to the world in these lines and facial characteristics.

The culprits most responsible for her older and more woeful look, Joey had no doubt, were the ugly abortion and the unworkable love affair with Jan. She could never tell the whole story to her parents, which made it harder for her to bear. She would have liked to get this story out and receive in turn their assurance that she had done the right thing—that she was not a murderess.

Joey had grown and matured. Her views had broadened beyond the homestead hearth, while those of her parents had remained fixed. She had become so accustomed to discussing diversified and controversial subjects with practically anyone, including almost total strangers, that it was weird indeed that she should have to hesitate when it came to her own parents.

The mirrored sad eyes she now wore were in mourning for her only love, Jan. How she grieved his loss still. She had spent the happiest times of her life with him, but also the saddest. The happy ones had sustained her. Listening to his guitar and violin playing, snorkelling together in the clear waters of the Mediterranean, or just ambling hand-in-hand in the hills. Joey knew she would carry his memory to the grave, but also her doubts. Did he really love her in his own funny way? Would he have married her in the end? She would never know now.

Her face of tomorrow was a well-kept secret, no matter how long or hard Joey stared in the glass. The future was veiled in mystery. She stroked the laughter lines around her eyes, for these were born of joy. She was not too upset either that at 27, age had taken only a small hold on her. Joey liked her self-image in spite of her terrible and horrifying mistakes. The more mature look suited her, and it gave her the courage she would need to face the unknown years ahead.

Retreat of Youth
Slipped through my fingers
Like quicksilver,
Faded—gone from view
Like a rainbow.
Elusive you were
As my shadow,

More valuable
Than a jewel.
I weep not your loss
As others do,
No plea in my eye
For recapture.
Contented am I
With my image—
That of an older
But wiser fool!

J. McP.

Shifting her attention away from the mirror, Joey's eyes lovingly embraced her room. The only bedroom she had truly known before she had left for college. Her yesterday's treasures were still scattered around. In the half-light, Joey looked towards the door as her mother came in to tell her that Jan was on the telephone and that she had post. Joey hurried out while her mother placed the letter bearing the addressee's name, Jean-Claude Monteux, on her dressing table. Once in the living room, Joey resolutely picked up the phone.

'Why, hello, Jan.'

'Darling Joey, I miss you so much.'

'Do you really, Jan? Have you nothing more important to say?'

Even now, Joey wondered if he regretted that she had left him. Was he calling to express a desire to come and be at her side again? Surely this would be proof enough of his love for her if he did. It would set her mind at peace.

'Please, dear God', Joey whispered to herself, 'have him say those words.'

'No, nothing special,' came Jan's non-committal reply.

Tears smarted Joey's eyes as she heard his voice coming so clearly as if from the next room, denying her what she most wanted to hear. An ache welled up in her soul, and she knew then she must prevent any such call from him in the future. Prolonging her grief would serve no good purpose.

'Jan, will you do something for me?'

'Anything,' he said light-heartedly.

'Promise never to contact me again?'

There was a long silence.

'Jan, Jan, are you still there?'

'I'm still here Joey,' he said sadly.

'Well, answer me, will you promise? Please, Jan, I need to know.'

'I promise, but I think you're making a big mistake.'

'No, not this time,' responded Joey with relief in her voice.

'Your three minutes are up', interrupted the operator, 'do you wish an extension, sir?'

'No, no, but don't cut me off till I've said goodbye,' Jan said with urgency.

'Go ahead, sir. Your party's still on the line.'

'Joey, I love you. I'll always be waiting.'

'Goodbye, Jan.'

Joey's final diary entry to this saga read as follows:

December 1959

Dear Diary, HOPE
Hope is a gentle zephyr,
That lifts our spirits high,
Guiding us o'er turbulence,
Wafting us through clear skies.
Trapped in becalmed seas of doubt,
Surrounded by dense fog,
Besieged by many failures,
We feel greatly lost.
'Tis then the gentle breeze blows,
Moving us on our way,
Filling our sails with brightness,
Clearing the fog away.
PS. JE ne regrette rien!

J. McP.

A Journey into Womanhood

Coral S. Jocic

Tuesday, January 29, 2019

☆☆☆☆☆

Review 1:

The book is centered by a vibrant character, Josephine McPhally which presents an interesting lesson that had notable repercussions. The book shines at capturing a reader's reflective mind with self- examining explorations. A delicate balance of quenching humor and ideas of society and a woman's bravery. A very likable character who is not afraid to live her life to the fullest!

Review 2:

An insightful book with a great storyline that deals with serious issues on love, gender roles, relationships and family pride. You could feel the internal turmoil the character is going through all throughout the book. Joey, was a pretty amusing character to read, but at the same time, you just can't help but feel sorry for her. It's amazing how the author made the transitions of the character and introduced it to a wider variety of maturity and greater knowledge of self and others.

Review 3:

The author did a great job at playing with a reader's emotions. The way she portrays the character's contradicting ideas about life and making decisions for yourself and others is breathtakingly impressive. Make no mistake, as this is no love story book! A book with a mixture of confusion and dedication where life proves to be the greatest lesson.

Review 4:

Times have really changed. Readers will grasp the importance of every women's role in the society today and the kind of ordeal and struggle they will do to gain respect in many areas of the world. As you go through the chapters of the book you won't really anticipate what's about to happen, you'll keep guessing and won't really know what to expect. The book isn't without flaws though, but, the author could've built up more each of the characters. Nonetheless, I would suggest anyone with an open mind for reality-dramas to go read this book.

Review 5:

An intriguing book about a woman who seeks for adventure to explore the world but met with life's unforeseen circumstances. The book tackles the issue of feminism and the value it adds to our society today as our status quo must be challenged. Though some readers might find the book cliché, the author did a great job to get the points across. A very well written book that created a fearless character out of Josephine McPhally!

Amazon Reviews

www.ingramcontent.com/pod-product-compliance
Lightning Source LLC
Chambersburg PA
CBHW071611030726
47598CB00001B/228

* 9 7 8 1 7 3 6 2 2 8 0 8 1 *